WITHOUT PRETENSE

Visit us at www.boldstrokesbooks.com

By the Author

A Reunion to Remember

Dawn's New Day

Without Pretense

WITHOUT PRETENSE

by

TJ Thomas

2019

WITHOUT PRETENSE

ISBN 13: 978-1-63555-173-0

This Trade Paperback Original Is Published By
Bold Strokes Books, Inc.
P.O. Box 249
Valley Falls, NY 12185

First Edition: February 2019

MAR 2 7 2019

Credits
Editor: Cindy Cresap
Production Design: Susan Ramundo
Cover Design By Melody Pond

Acknowledgments

Tucked away in the Berkshire Hills of Western Massachusetts is Tanglewood, the summer home of the Boston Symphony Orchestra and one of my happy places. It is a haven away from the hustle and bustle of life. My wyf and I love to go to Tanglewood during the summer. Under a starry sky, and sometimes even the threat of rain, we stake a claim to a picnic-sized spot and listen to amazing music. During one of those summer evenings this story was born. As we lay on a blanket and enjoyed the sounds of a solo violinist, Elle said, "You should write a story about her." For the rest of the performance, we went back and forth—me asking questions, Elle positing what might happen next. As we drove home, the questions continued and the beginning of the story was set.

Not surprisingly, the story begins in Tanglewood. At the time, I did not know where else it would take us, but it turned out to be a fun ride. While writing this book, I fell a bit in love with both characters. Ava and Bianca are people I would want to know and count as friends. I hope you enjoy them as well. I am forever grateful to Tanglewood for both the inspiration and the memories we make there. If you're ever in the area, I encourage you to visit. It is quite lovely.

Most of my characters are influenced in some way by people I know. Their characteristics and tendencies grow out of small moments. In this case, Ava was influenced by our daughter, Kate, and my eldest sister, Anne. Anne is the happiest person I know. She takes nothing for granted and deeply appreciates every small act—as every person with Down's syndrome I know does. Anne loves people, life, and food—oh, the food! She is easily excitable and pleased by the smallest things. We can all learn much from Anne; I know I have. Ava was modeled after her in those ways.

From Kate, Ava inherited an intense interest in the physical world around her. One afternoon, on our way home from a daily excursion to the park, our progress was delayed by frequent stops for our granddaughter, Nourah, to experience the tactile world around her. We stopped to feel the petals of a flower, rub the bark of a tree, scratch the clay of a brick, and Nourah's favorite, pet the long fur of a fluffy orange cat. I watched with amazement as Kate took the time and care to introduce Nourah to the world through touch, texture, and color. This exchange was amazing in its simplicity and the wonder and excitement it garnered from Nourah. It was astonishing for its innocence and it has remained with me.

Many aspects of writing are solitary, but the process of getting a novel into the world and a reader's hands takes a lot of people. I am thankful to all the folks at Bold Strokes Books who are a part of making this happen. I am consistently amazed by the work done by Sandra Lowe and Radclyffe. Their tireless work keeps quality novels in the works. Thank you to Melody Pond for the beautiful cover. To my editor, Cindy Cresap, who keeps the mistakes I make out of the final product. Thank you for making this a better book, again.

Sharing your words can be difficult, especially before they are polished and refined. I am fortunate to have people I can trust with my works-in-progress. Many thanks go to Aurora Rey, Jackie Katz, and Maeve Howett. Your feedback, suggestions, and encouragement were invaluable.

To my wyf, Elle, who inspired this story and once again read every version. Your input, support, and love…no thanks will ever be enough. After eleven years, I'm still trying to piece together how I'm lucky enough to have won your heart. I cherish it and you—forever and always. Our children are grown now and living their own lives. Our grandchildren are growing so fast it's hard to keep up. All the moments and memories, no matter how long we're together…it will never be enough.

Finally, to you, the reader, thank you for choosing this book. Thank you for choosing romance. Without you, none of this would matter. Now, I leave you with this story.

Dedication

Elle,

I love you way more than that.

PROLOGUE

Ava Wellington stepped outside into the warm sunlight and took a deep, cleansing breath. She hated being cooped up. It was a necessary evil at times given the nature of her profession. Today, she had time before rehearsal. So she escaped to explore the grounds, as she did as often as possible. It was a gorgeous summer day, and she wanted to enjoy the nature that surrounded her professional home for the week. Rain or shine, she loved the fresh piney air and being surrounded by towering trees, fragrant flowers, and the immense natural beauty here.

She pulled her hair into a loose ponytail, took off her sandals to feel the grass between her toes, and meandered toward her favorite spot on the grounds of Tanglewood. This little piece of heaven tucked away in the Berkshire Mountains of Western Massachusetts never failed to soothe her soul. Distracted by the majestic trees under the brilliant blue sky, she didn't see the lone figure sitting on the bench she was heading for until she was nearly on top of her.

She walked wide to cross her sightline so she didn't startle her. She debated whether to approach the woman. She paused, transfixed by her beauty. With naturally bronzed smooth skin, high cheekbones, a small straight nose, and full lips, she was striking, and Ava was drawn to her. The sadness etched deep into her features caught Ava off guard. She stared intensely, unable to look away. The woman's large, dark brown eyes appeared focused on something far in the distance. It tugged at Ava's heart and compelled her forward.

Settling onto the seat, Ava asked, "Are you okay?"

The woman looked at the horizon. She didn't respond. Ava didn't know if she was being ignored or hadn't been heard. She wondered if she should leave, but she couldn't. She wanted to help. She laid her hand on the woman's forearm. Ava didn't attempt to console her. She simply took a soft handkerchief from her shorts pocket and gently laid it on the woman's lap.

The woman looked down and picked it up, and then she went back to staring into the distance. She began to cry. As tears streamed down her face, crying turned to sobbing. Her shoulders shook, and her body seemed to shrink. Despair poured from her, and Ava couldn't do anything except sit with her. After her crying subsided, she mopped her face with the borrowed cloth and offered it back to Ava.

Ava shook her head gently. "Keep it," she said just above a whisper.

"Thank you."

"Are you going to be okay?"

"Probably. Eventually, but no time soon."

"I can be a good listener if you want to talk."

"My wife died four months ago in a plane crash."

"I cannot imagine how hard that must be."

"It's devastating. I'm still struggling. I have no idea what I'm doing without her."

Ava ached for this woman's loss. There had to be some way she could help. "Do you want to tell me about her?"

"Karen was bold and brave, stubborn and ornery. She had a head for business that was inspirational. She was the youngest vice president ever at her company. Her sense of humor was sharp. She made me laugh all the time. She was also pregnant. We'd just found out the month before that we were going to have a little girl." Her voice faltered and she shook her head ever so slightly as the tears began again. "I miss her so much."

Ava wrapped her arm around the grieving woman's shoulders and pulled her close. She laid her head on Ava's shoulder and the tears turned back to sobbing. Ava wished with all she was that the woman in her arms was not hurting. She wasn't usually so comfortable with emotion, hers or anyone else's, but this felt comfortable, helpful even.

They sat in silence until the sobs subsided. Ava sat still, offering the only thing she could, comfort in the form of a gentle touch and company. Eventually, the woman caught her breath, but she didn't move either. Ava knew rehearsal time was drawing near, and if Ava wasn't there on time, someone would come looking for her. She cleared her throat softly. "I'm sorry, but I have to go soon. I have an appointment."

The woman raised her head and met Ava's gaze. Her eyes were red and puffy, and her face was still damp with tears. She was breathtakingly beautiful. She wiped her face with the handkerchief and pulled away. She sat upright and regained control. "I'm sorry. I didn't mean for this to happen. I certainly didn't mean to keep you."

"Don't apologize. I was exactly where I wanted to be," Ava said.

"You mean that, don't you?"

"I do."

"You may be the oddest woman I've ever met."

"I've been called worse." Ava smiled.

"Oh no, I didn't mean that in a bad way. I've just never met anyone so willing to console a perfect stranger," she said.

"I'm not always so comfortable with people."

"You fooled me."

"It was easy with you."

"I've also never met anyone that carries a handkerchief."

"I always have at least one on me. I use them to clean my violin."

"Oh, you're a musician."

"Yes, and unfortunately, I need to get to rehearsal."

"You should go."

Neither of them moved.

"I'd much rather stay here and talk to you, but duty calls." She held out her hand. "I'm Ava."

"Bianca," she said, taking Ava's hand gently. "Thank you for the ear and the shoulder. And the handkerchief."

"You're welcome." There was so much more Ava wanted to say, but nothing else seemed appropriate given all Bianca had shared and all she'd recently lost. Ava stood. "Will you be staying for the show this evening?"

"Maybe. I was thinking about it. I'm not sure I'll be up for it."

"I would love for you to come as my guest."

"Oh, no, I couldn't do that. I've already kept you."

"How about this, I'll leave a ticket at the box office for you. If you decide to come, great, if not, I understand."

"You don't need to do that, really."

"I want to." Ava took Bianca's hand in hers. "Thank you for today."

Bianca cocked her head. "Why are you thanking me?"

"You trusted me enough to tell me why you were sad even though you don't know me."

"Maybe that's why. It all spilled out of me."

"I hope to see you again, Bianca."

Bianca wandered around her living room. She was debating whether she should go to the show. Exhausted from crying when she returned home, she slept solidly for an hour. Now refreshed from a quick shower, she was agitated. As strange as the time she'd spent with Ava had been, she felt safe and comforted in her arms. The thought of drowning in her melancholy thoughts all evening was enough to compel her to pull on a summer dress and head back to Tanglewood.

As she reached the ticket window, she looked hopelessly at the woman behind the glass. "Umm, I'm Bianca. Ava said she would leave a ticket for me." She didn't have Ava's last name, and she hadn't given Ava hers. With so little information, how would the ticket office be able to find the ticket? Never once did it occur to her that Ava may have forgotten to leave it for her. She had said she would and Bianca believed her.

The woman smiled brightly. "Of course, we have it right here."

Bianca let out a sigh of relief. "Thank you very much."

"You're welcome. Enjoy the show."

Bianca walked to the gate and handed her ticket to the man there. "Can you tell me how I get to my seat?"

He glanced briefly at the ticket. "Head for the Shed and any usher will be able to direct you."

"Thank you."

Bianca had never sat inside the Shed for a show. She had wandered through it on occasion when she and Karen came to shows early, but they had always gotten lawn seats and sat in camp chairs under the stars. She had never been inside the open-sided, covered building that housed the stage where the musicians performed, when the stage was set. It was exciting. As she followed the usher closer and closer to the stage, she grew wary. He pointed to a seat in the center of the third row. "Are you sure that's the right seat?"

"Yes, ma'am." He handed her back her ticket. "See for yourself."

Bianca compared her ticket to the seat numbers. There was no denying it. She was getting emotional all over again and didn't know why. She nodded to the usher. "Thank you." She made her way to her seat and kept her tears in check. Who was Ava that she could so casually give away one of the best seats in the house?

"Ava, darling, you need to sit still if you don't want me to pull your hair out."

Ava sighed and tried to relax. "Sorry, Steven, it's been a weird day." She shifted in the chair.

"Don't worry, hon. A couple more hours and it'll be over."

Ava grinned at Steven. Her hair and makeup artist was the closest thing she had to a best friend. "Thanks. I invited a woman to the show tonight and I'm anxious to see if she decided to come."

"Oh, hon, why didn't you just say something? Let's take a peek."

"Really?"

"Yes. There's nothing here that won't keep for two minutes. Come on." He pulled her out of the chair and marched her down the hall to the stage door where she could peek through the window and see the audience gathering for the show.

Ava felt a little rebellious, standing in her robe peering out at the crowd. She breathed a sigh of relief when she spotted Bianca in the audience. "She's here," she said quietly.

Steven crowded her to see through the window. "Where?"

"Third row, center."

"Ooh, the hot Latina?"

"Her name is Bianca."

"She doesn't look like your usual type." Steven raised an eyebrow in question.

Ava bristled. "What do you mean by that?"

"Oh, hon, I didn't mean anything. I was just giving you a hard time. I guess it's your lucky night."

"It's not like that."

"Why ever not? As previously stated, she's hot."

Ava sighed. She didn't want to betray Bianca's confidences. "It's complicated. I met her this afternoon. It seemed like she needed a distraction so I invited her to the show."

"Okay." Steven had known her for years and probably suspected there was more to the story, but he let it go. "Speaking of distractions, we need to finish getting you ready."

Ava glanced out at the audience, finding Bianca one last time, then she followed Steven back to her dressing room.

Bianca looked everywhere at once trying to take it all in. As the musicians took their places, she tried to find Ava in the crowd. She didn't see her, but all the women had their hair down and Ava's had been up that afternoon. Maybe she had missed her. There were a couple of violinists she couldn't see clearly. She had to be back there somewhere. Everyone was in black and white. The men wore tuxedos—black trousers and white jackets. The women seemed to take more liberty with their attire. All wore black slacks or skirts. But their white tops were a variety of blouses, tuxedo shirts, or light sweaters.

Karen would have loved this. Bianca caught herself as the pain pierced her heart. She should probably leave. She had been wrong thinking she could be around people tonight. She had been so distracted by everything on stage, the seats around her had filled without her being aware. In the next moment, the music started. She didn't want to interrupt the orchestra or the audience. She took a few deeps breaths and reined in the pain and brought it to a manageable level. After a while, she stopped thinking about Karen. She stopped looking for Ava. She immersed herself in the rich, beautiful music and stopped thinking altogether.

The symphony played for about thirty minutes going from one song to the next with easy, smooth transitions. When the music stopped, Bianca clapped loudly. Her spirit was lighter than it had been since Karen's accident. She listened intently as the conductor introduced the soloist for the evening's performance. "Ladies and gentlemen, please give your warmest Tanglewood welcome to Ava Wellington."

Bianca was so surprised when he reached the end of his primer, she forgot to clap. When the door on the right side of the stage opened and Ava walked through in a long, sleeveless, cobalt gown, she was mesmerized. Bianca watched as Ava moved across the stage. Ava had been in shorts and bare feet, with her hair in a ponytail, when she'd bared her soul to her hours before. Now she stood center stage transformed into an elegant, sophisticated, world-renowned violinist. Her golden hair fell to her shoulders in soft waves. Her shoulders were bare keeping her arms free to play her instrument without impediment. Ava bowed slightly to the audience, and her gaze met Bianca's. A hint of a smile raised the corners of her mouth. She stood tall, lifted her chin, and tucked the violin between her chin and shoulder. She briefly closed her eyes as she began to play.

Once Ava's gaze left her, Bianca realized she was holding her breath. She exhaled and wondered if there was any way this day could get stranger. She fixed her gaze on Ava, drifting between her face and her long, slender hands. The music she played was lovely.

Tender and heart wrenching. Bianca felt like Ava was playing all the emotions she had shared that afternoon. Bianca experienced the music as she never had before. It was exhausting and exhilarating. She felt exposed but not uncomfortable. Somehow, Ava was sharing her sorrow with the audience and Bianca felt freer, lighter. Ava alternated playing by herself and playing with the orchestra. Bianca could have listened to her play all night.

Ava's violin solos were wonderful. The music and Ava's incredible skill took Bianca's breath away. The emotion Ava conveyed while she played was inspiring in its beauty. Bianca was riveted. She couldn't have moved if she needed to, and at times she realized she was holding her breath, waiting to exhale with the music.

When Bianca had seen Ava on the bench, she had taken her for much younger than she now seemed. The fresh-faced young woman from earlier was transformed into an elegant and experienced virtuoso. Bianca couldn't have been so far off in guessing her age. Ava must be some sort of prodigy. When the concert reached a crescendo and the music stopped, Bianca leapt to her feet with everyone else and clapped loudly for Ava and the orchestra. Then she slumped back into her seat, breathless and exhausted.

Bianca reflected on the very strange day that had unfolded. She wasn't likely to forget it any time soon. Bianca's emotions had been on a roller coaster all day and this evening was entirely unexpected. As the crowd thinned, she remained seated. There was nowhere else she needed to be, and she wanted to sit and let her emotions subside. She wanted to be present in this moment as it was the first time since she'd received word of Karen's death that she felt anything other than anger or despair.

A well-groomed man in a pink blazer approached her. "Bianca?"

"Yes?"

He held out a single white rose. "My name is Steven. I'm a friend of Ava's. She asked me to give this to you. She's hoping you will come back and say hello."

Bianca took the flower and couldn't resist breathing in its rich scent. "Yes, of course. Where is back?"

"Just come with me."

Bianca trailed Steven through the throngs of musicians in the hallway. When Steven stopped outside a door with a gold plaque, Bianca was inexplicably nervous. What would she possibly say to this woman of contradictions? Ava had been so composed on stage but had been so compassionate that afternoon. She was an enigma, and Bianca felt vulnerable and exposed. She grabbed Steven's shoulder. "Wait."

He paused, his hand inches from knocking.

"I should just go. Will you tell Ava thank you for me?"

Steven frowned. "I could, but I'm not going to. All she wants to do is say hi. There's no pressure here."

Bianca took a deep breath and squared her shoulders. "Right. Okay."

Steven knocked and opened the door swiftly so Bianca didn't have time to change her mind. He gave Ava a brief hug. "Great performance, darling," he said as he swept Bianca into the room.

"Thanks." She hugged him back, but her eyes were on Bianca. "Will you give us a minute, Steven?"

"Sure, hon."

Once he left, Ava appeared shy, like she was as nervous as Bianca. Bianca forcefully expelled a breath, trying to release the tension that had swelled inside her. "That was fabulous. You're amazing."

The corners of Ava's mouth lifted. "I'm glad you enjoyed it."

"I did. It was so…" Bianca searched for the right word. "Expressive."

"Thank you." Ava paused. "Listen, I have to stick around for a while after the show to sign autographs and stuff. After that I was, um, wondering if you'd like to get coffee with me."

Bianca hesitated.

"Just coffee. I would like to get to know you better."

"I'm sorry, but it's been a long day and I can't." Bianca caught her breath as pain quickly passed through Ava's eyes, but it was gone so quickly she wondered if she imagined it.

Ava's smile didn't quite reach her eyes. "I understand. Thank you for coming to the show."

"Thank you so much for the ticket. The music was beautiful, but I need to go." Bianca didn't move.

"Wait. Before you do, I'd like to give you something."

"You've already given me so much."

"No, I haven't. Please wait one minute." Ava turned to her dressing table and picked a CD from a stack by the mirror and grabbed the Sharpie next to the pile. She dashed off a note and closed the case. She held it out to Bianca. "A little something to remember me by."

Bianca took it and held it to her chest. She looked directly into Ava's eyes. "I will treasure it, but I won't need a reminder. Thank you…for everything."

"You're welcome, Bianca. I hope we meet again someday."

Bianca left quickly and pulled the door shut behind her.

"What a very strange day." Ava sighed. As she looked around the room, she felt lonely.

CHAPTER ONE

Two Years Later

Ava slammed through the doors and burst out into the blinding sunshine. She was seething with anger and needed to try to walk it off. Hank had lied to her. He had been her agent and manager for three years, and she wasn't naïve enough to think he was always honest. He was an agent, after all. But this was the first time she'd caught him in an outright lie. She had been very clear when she'd told him she was not interested in having a biography written.

He had disregarded her wishes, gone behind her back, and hired a writer to follow her around for the next six months. There was no way that was going to happen. No way. She would not be traipsed after by some pale, nerdy author who got his rocks off peering into the personal lives of public figures. She would put a stop to this. Nothing good came from reacting. She needed to calm down and respond.

Since Hank hired BJ Vega, whoever the hell he was, he would just have to tell the guy his services were no longer required. She should just fire his ass. That would show him who was boss. But she didn't like making decisions in anger, so she walked across the grounds of Tanglewood. She needed time and space to think things through.

She didn't realize she had a specific destination in mind until she saw the bench under the giant pine tree. Two years ago she'd had the strangest experience on that bench. Bianca. She had known her for just a few hours, and yet the memories of that encounter haunted her. She hoped she had found a way through the pain and loss that was so raw that afternoon. Ava sat on the bench, her back to the Shed just as she had with Bianca. She thought back to their last minutes together, to the note she wrote in the CD case she gave her.

She'd written her number down, but Bianca never called. As disappointed as she'd been, she couldn't fault her. She knew Bianca was overwhelmed with grief when they'd met. All she'd wanted to do was help. Clearly, Bianca wasn't ready. She thought about her often, but every time she returned to Tanglewood, the memory of the time she spent with Bianca on that bench was more present in her mind.

Ava was sure she had conjured Bianca when she appeared in her sightline and was walking toward her. As the image of Bianca strode closer, her certainty wavered. Bianca being here brightened Ava's whole day and she forgot Hank and the book. She even forgot she had rehearsal and a show later. All of those things flew from her mind as Bianca sat on the bench beside her.

"Bianca, please tell me you're really here and this isn't just a dream."

Bianca laughed and placed her hand on Ava's thigh. "You remember me after all this time?"

Ava's stomach clenched at the warm, soft hand on her leg and the beautiful sound of Bianca's soft accent. "I've never forgotten you or the time we spent together."

Bianca's eyebrows drew together in consternation, and she clasped her hands in her lap. "How is it that we have known one another, in reality, for just a few hours and I completely believe you?"

"I don't really understand it myself, but I feel a…connection to you."

"I feel it too."

"Then how come you never called?" Ava blurted the question before she could stop it. She didn't mean to put Bianca on the spot, but the question had haunted her for two years.

Bianca pursed her lips and gazed into the distance as though searching for the answer. She turned to Ava. "I wanted to. I picked up the phone so many times, but I couldn't do it. I was so overwhelmed with my feelings. I didn't want to drag you into all that."

"Did you ever think I could have helped? That I wanted to help?"

"Yes. I knew you would have. I couldn't let you."

"Why?"

"Because I wanted you to so much."

"I don't understand."

Bianca put her hand back on Ava's thigh. "I needed to do it on my own. My own time, my own process. The only woman I had ever loved died four months before we met. You made me feel safe and secure. I felt like I could tell you all my secrets. I wanted to get to know you, but I felt like I was betraying Karen. It was so confusing. I didn't know what to do or how to handle all those feelings at once. So, I did the most logical thing I could." Bianca shrugged. "I ran away, or more accurately, I buried my head in the sand and avoided you until I could better deal with everything that was happening.

"By the time things settled down and I got a handle on my emotions, months had gone by. It didn't seem right to call you out of the blue. I was sure you wouldn't even remember me. So I played your CD often and thought of you and that afternoon we spent together. You will never know how much you helped me that day. How much your beautiful music soothed me during countless nights."

"What made you come back?"

"You! I wanted to see you. I felt such a strong connection to you two years ago. I had to find out if it was still there and if you felt it too."

Ava ran her thumb over the top of Bianca's hand. "I did. I do."

"Me too."

"What do you want to do about it?"

"I have no idea. I didn't expect things to move this fast," Bianca said.

Ava took Bianca's hand in hers. "Will you come to the show tonight and then come out with me after?"

"I would love to, but there's something else you should know first."

"Are you single, available, and interested in getting to know me better?"

"Yes, yes, and definitely, but—"

"Nothing else matters right now. Come to the show and we'll talk later."

"Okay."

"I should get to rehearsal. I'll leave you a ticket. Don't disappear. Please." Ava stood and Bianca rose with her.

"I won't."

"Before I go, I need to…" Ava leaned down and touched her lips to Bianca's. She only touched her with her mouth, gently sliding her lips over Bianca's. When Bianca's mouth opened, Ava softly slipped her tongue inside and moaned. She pulled back and lifted her head. Bianca's eyes were almost black with desire. "Even better than I imagined," Ava said.

"I believe I will enjoy this getting to know you phase very much."

As Ava walked back to the Shed, she wondered if she was moving too fast. She didn't want Bianca to retreat. On the other hand, she had been thinking about what she would do if she ever saw Bianca again. Going forward, she needed to remember to take it more slowly and make sure Bianca was comfortable. She was special. This was different.

Alone in her dressing room after rehearsal, Ava struggled to wrap her head around everything that happened that afternoon. She'd spent rehearsal on autopilot, her mind completely consumed by Bianca, who had reappeared out of a daydream. Her reverie was interrupted by a knock on the door.

"Come in." She glanced over to see who was there to see her. "Go away. I'm still mad at you."

Hank didn't listen. He came into the room. "Come on, Ava, you can't stay mad. This is happening. You need to get used to the idea."

"No. I don't. And right now, I need to concentrate on this show. You need to leave. Now."

Hank stared at her for several seconds. "I'll check in with you after the show. I'll bring BJ back to meet you."

He was gone before Ava could find something to throw at him, but boy, did she want to. She didn't usually behave this way. She was passionate in all aspects of her life, especially when it came to her music, women, and food. But rarely did she lose her temper. She did not want her biography written. It could tear her family apart and it would all be her fault. Luckily, before she wandered too far down that slippery slope of memories, she was distracted by another knock.

"What?" she snapped.

Steven poked his head in. "I just saw Hank leave. Is it safe to come in?"

Ava couldn't help but smile. Steven was the only one brave or foolish enough to risk facing her in one of her rare bad moods. "Safe enough for you."

Steven came in, closed the door behind him, and leaned against it. "Where did you run off to before rehearsal?"

Ava moved to the chair so Steven could do her makeup before he did her hair. "I went for a walk so I could think about all the ways I wanted to punish Hank for what he did."

"That's fair, but why don't you just tell Hank why you don't want your biography written? He'd probably understand."

"My private life is none of his business. It should be enough for me to tell him I don't want it done. He should respect that."

"I agree with you. As for your private life, do you think you'll ever tire of keeping the secret? Maybe it's time to let it go and be free of it."

Ava met his eyes in the mirror. "Maybe you're right, but aside from telling you more than a decade ago when I was blitzed out of my head, it's not something I've shared with anyone outside my family. That's a hard thing to change."

"I get that," he said as he smoothed the sponge across her cheekbones, blending color and blush.

"I know you do. This is too much before a performance. Let's talk about something else."

"What do you have in mind?"

"I was pleasantly surprised today when I ran into an old friend."

"Oh?"

He could say so much with one syllable. He was the only person she'd ever told about Bianca. More than once, he had patiently listened to her bemoan that Bianca had never called.

Ava laughed. "Bianca found me on the grounds. At first I thought she was a figment of my fantasies, but there she was in the flesh."

Steven bent down in front of Ava working to apply just the right stage makeup. "Do you want me to hate her or forgive her?"

She looked directly at him. "Forgive her. Since we have a date after the show."

"Okay, hon. If that's what you want, you got it."

It was just that simple with Steven. He probably had a thousand questions, but he trusted Ava and did as she asked. Ava appreciated him more every day.

"It is. Can you do me a favor at intermission?"

"Of course. Anything."

Ava loved being on stage at Tanglewood more than a lot of the venues she played. The summer home of the Boston Symphony Orchestra was a unique setting. The Koussevitzky Music Shed only had walls in the area around the stage. The covered audience area was an open structure with steel columns supporting the roof. During the day you could see from the stage out to the grass beyond the last seat. She appreciated seeing the thousands of people who peppered the grass in lawn seats. They set up elaborate picnics while they listened to the music. Even during the night concerts, she knew they were there and could feel their energy.

Tonight, as she played, her mind wasn't on the crowd and how much they were enjoying the show. Her performance tonight was for one special woman. Bianca had come back into her life, and she wasn't going to let her get away so easily this time. She looked for her in the audience, and her heart warmed when their gazes met.

Knowing Bianca was there listening to the music she played made Ava feel close to her.

Ava had to be careful. She couldn't get her hopes up too high. After all, she barely knew Bianca. Clearly, they had a strong connection, at least from her perspective, and Bianca had said the same that afternoon. But what did she really know about her other than that she was a widow? Maybe all the fantasies she'd created over the last two years were best left to her imagination.

After Ava left for rehearsal, Bianca wandered around the grounds, lingering at a clutch of tall pines and then gazing out at the Berkshires that rise on the horizon over the tall hedges at the back of the property. She had been nervous that if Ava remembered her at all, she wouldn't forgive her for disappearing. Ava made it easier than she thought possible to reconnect. She had wanted to tell her why she was there, but Ava hadn't given her a chance. She had only wanted to make sure the two of them could get together later.

She hoped when Ava discovered the other reason Bianca reappeared in her life she wouldn't send her packing. She really did want to learn more about the talented Ava Wellington and not simply because it was her job now.

As she watched Ava play, the music from her violin flowed over Bianca like a waterfall surrounding her with sound and beauty. The emotion Ava conveyed with her instrument could easily consume or soothe her by equal measure. Hers was a singular talent and Bianca was intrigued by Ava. She wanted to get to know the woman behind the music. She had come back, at the invitation of Ava's manager, to write her biography.

Would Ava feel betrayed that Bianca hadn't told her the real reason she had come back into her life? She certainly had not anticipated the kiss Ava had given her that afternoon. That kiss still had Bianca stirred up and her lips tingling. It had been a sweet, tender kiss, but Bianca was absolutely sure there was nothing simple about it.

CHAPTER TWO

Ava stared Hank down as they faced off in her dressing room after the show. "Why did you hire a biographer when I'd explicitly told you not to?"

"I still don't understand why you are so upset. This will be a good boost for your career. It will get your name out there."

"First of all, my name doesn't need to be out there more than it already is. I don't need more recognition or fame. I just want to play my music. But more importantly, you don't know anything about me or my life. You have no right to hire a biographer without my knowledge. I told you I didn't want a biography written and that should have been the end of the story. Why did you go behind my back like this?"

"Because you wouldn't listen to me and you need this."

"Why do I *need* my biography written?"

"Ava, at thirty-three, you're just another violinist. I'm sorry if that's harsh, but it's true. You're no longer the young prodigy solo violinist headlining shows at seventeen. People don't see you as special anymore. But you still are. You're still relevant and you're still a genius on the violin. People need to see that in you and this is the way to make them invested in who you are now. You said yourself just last month that there needs to be more positive lesbian role models for children. Think of how many young lives you might positively impact if we get your story out there. Not the tabloid version of you, but the real you."

Hank's answer surprised her. Ava had said that about role models, but she didn't think Hank was actually listening to her at the time. The problem was she didn't want her life story told. At least not all of it. The thought more than terrified her. There was only one thing that had ever scared her more in her entire life. That was when she found out she was pregnant at sixteen and she had to figure out what to do about it.

"On top of that, you're always excited to share classical music with new people. You love teaching young musicians. This could be an avenue to do more of that as well," Hank said.

He was very convincing and made excellent points. There was a reason she had hired him to be her negotiator in business matters. Still, nothing he said or could say changed the fact that Ava had a secret and she would do anything to keep it hidden. If the truth came out, it would hurt the people she loved the most. She had to admit, though, a lot of good could come out of this if it was handled the right way. "I control the narrative," she said with resolution.

Hank looked pained.

"What's the problem?" Ava asked.

Hank bounced from foot to foot and looked like he wasn't going to answer until he finally did. "It's just that this won't work as a fluff piece. Vega has a reputation for writing compelling and honest stories. Vega's biographies move more people because they're so real."

"So find someone else to write the damn thing," Ava practically yelled. She took a deep breath. She needed to hear what Hank had to say. This was too important to fly off the handle. She struggled to keep her wits about her and figure out a way to either get out of this or make it work.

"We can't. Vega is the best. You want the best, don't you?"

Ava doubted she did in this case, but how could she explain that to Hank without telling him why? He wouldn't believe her without a valid reason. He knew her penchant for wanting the best of everything.

"Vega's written biographies on celebrities that revealed drug and drinking problems nobody knew about before. Finding the untold story and bringing it to light. Vega also writes a compassionate story, which makes the readers sympathetic. It's what makes the books so popular. Do you remember the Etheridge biography that came out last year?" Hank asked.

"Vaguely." Ava hedged. In truth she had read it three times. She wasn't all that interested in Etheridge herself. Enough to have picked it up she supposed. But the writing had captivated her. The story was so well done, she found herself returning to it every so often.

"Well, I'm sure you remember what a boon it was to her flailing career."

Not what she'd been thinking about. Reading that book always made her wonder about the author. Probably not the point of the story, but she did all the same. Hank was looking at her expectantly. "Sure. She seemed to be everywhere after that story came out. She was booked on all the late night shows, the daytime ones too, and I remember hearing her entire tour this past spring sold out."

"Vega wrote that story."

Some part of Ava must have known that. But right now, she had a bigger problem. There was no way she could let her secret come to light. "So, you don't think this guy will play ball and keep out the parts I don't want talked about?"

"No, I don't think *she* will. What do you have to hide anyway? You were a musical prodigy and you're already out as a lesbian. What else is she going to find? It's not like you have some deep dark past drug addiction I don't know about, right?"

Ava didn't answer him right away. She was stuck on his use of the feminine pronoun. Now she was intrigued. "BJ Vega is a woman?"

Hank smiled as if he'd just laid down his last card to win a big jackpot. He seemed to think he had her now. "She is."

That shouldn't make a difference. Ava still didn't want her biography written, at least not a tell-all. But somehow the fact BJ was female did matter to her. At the very least she wanted to meet the woman who wrote such compelling stories. Perhaps she could convince or charm BJ into not digging beyond what she wanted her to see. Because Hank did have a point about a biography being able to make her relevant for a younger generation, and that was important to her.

"Okay. I will agree to a meeting, but I'm not saying yes yet."

"If you don't do this, people will forget who you are. That is if they ever knew who you were in the first place."

"Ouch. Harsh."

"Look, my point is, with Vega's reputation of telling relevant, revealing stories, her books soar to the top of the bestseller list as soon as they're released. She can make you a household name. Once that happens, you can make classical music accessible to the masses."

"I said I would meet with her."

"Ava, you need this."

Ava glared at him, still not happy with how he went about things. "I will decide what I need. But I will consider your recommendation."

Before Hank could respond, they were interrupted by a knock on the door.

"Come in," Ava said.

Bianca entered and saw Ava had changed from the elegant gown she wore on stage into jeans and a button-down casual shirt over a cotton T-shirt. Hank stood a few feet from her. The tension in the room made Bianca feel as though she'd interrupted an intense conversation. "Sorry, I can come back," Bianca said.

"Wait," Ava said.

Hank held out his hand and waved her over. "Nonsense, your timing is perfect."

Bianca watched Ava's expression change from warm and welcoming to one of confusion with Hank's words.

"Ava, I would like you to meet BJ Vega," Hank said.

Bianca couldn't read Ava's normally expressive features. She still had a job to do. She held out her hand. "Ms. Wellington, it's a pleasure to meet you."

Ava stared at Bianca's hand and then raised her gaze to Bianca's, but she said nothing.

After several tense moments of awkward silence, Ava finally looked at Hank. "Why don't you give BJ and me a few minutes?"

Bianca heard the hard emphasis Ava placed on her initials and cringed. But at least she would have a moment alone with her to try to explain.

Hank headed for the door. Bianca stepped out of his way and he was gone.

Bianca moved no closer to Ava. The ball was in Ava's court. She wasn't even sure she was still in the game.

"BJ?" Ava's voice was a mixture of derision and hurt.

Bianca didn't want to think about those things. "Yes, it's my professional name."

"You're a biographer?" Ava sounded stunned.

"I am. Unfortunately, given what I learned from Hank after I saw you this afternoon, I'm now aware you didn't know he hired me."

"That's true. He did it without my knowledge."

"I'm sorry to hear that. Hank led me to believe you were on board with this project."

"It seems that Hank has a lot to answer for. Why didn't you tell me you were here for work when I saw you earlier?"

"I told you the truth. I'm here because I want to get to know you better. I tried to tell you the rest, but you said nothing else mattered except that I wanted to go out with you. Had I known you didn't know about me, I would have tried harder. I took you at your word."

Ava put her hands in her pockets. "Do you still want to go out with me tonight?"

"Yes."

Ava took a step toward her. "Even if…"

"Let me stop you right there." This time Bianca took a step toward Ava. "My answer is still yes. No matter how many caveats you put on our date. I want to spend time with you."

Ava was within touching distance as she studied Bianca for several more moments. "Then let's get out of here."

❖

After following Bianca home so her car wouldn't be locked on the grounds, Ava drove them a few miles down the road. She pulled her Wrangler into the parking lot of the Wet Whistle and turned to Bianca. "Ready?"

"Should we talk about earlier?"

"Later. Right now, I just want to have some fun." Ava opened the door for Bianca. Once again, she held out her hand for Bianca to take and they walked into the dimly lit bar.

The bouncer, John, gripped Ava in a tight hug. "Where you been, Ava?"

Ava returned the fierceness of the hug. "Around, but I missed your face, so I thought I'd come by. John, meet Bianca." John gave Bianca an equally tight hug and welcomed her. Ava and Bianca wound their way through the raucous horde of humanity on the dance floor. Ava was stopped more than once and similar exchanges took place.

By the time she reached the bar, Bianca's head was spinning. "Wow. You sure have a lot of friends here."

The smile that lit Ava's face was telling. "It's been too long since I've seen them."

"Why so long?"

Ava shrugged and looked around before answering. "Well, with my travel schedule I'm not in this area all that much. Would you like a drink?"

Bianca considered. "Why don't we dance first and then get drinks when we need a breather."

"I love that plan. Come on."

Ava took Bianca's hand and led her to the middle of the room. There wasn't a dance floor per se. People just seemed to dance wherever they could find a couple feet of space. The energy was high and the classic rock music was loud. It wasn't an environment conducive to talking, so they moved to the music, looking into one another's eyes.

When the music slowed, Bianca moved into Ava's arms without any hesitation. Their bodies fit together perfectly. She was too close to meet her eyes, but also afraid of what her own might reveal in that moment. So she laid her head on Ava's shoulder and moved with her to the music.

When the band took a break, Ava led Bianca back to the bar. Moments after the bartender handed them their drinks, the lead singer picked Ava up from behind and crushed her in a bear hug. "Hey, stranger, what are you doing down here? You have to play a set with us."

Bianca looked between the two of them. Ava introduced Bianca to him and quickly explained. "Sometimes I play drums with the band."

It took some convincing from the rest of the band, but eventually Ava was ushered up to the stage where she took her place behind the drums. She counted off, and the band launched into the next set seamlessly. Ava played the drums with skill and precision.

Bianca had so many questions. She had been hired to write a biography of Ava Wellington, world-class violinist. Where did this drummer fit into the story? Or did she? Not that Ava was all that happy about her life story being written in the first place. Bianca suspected if the two of them didn't have a history, however brief it was, she wouldn't be here now. Ava would not have acquiesced to her manager's wishes, and Bianca would have been fired from her position of biographer before the job even started.

She shook off her thoughts and refocused on Ava. She looked so natural behind the drum set. Maybe even more at home than she was on the Tanglewood stage in front of thousands of people holding the violin that had been a part of her life for so long. Bianca tried to make sense of the divergent parts of the woman she had really only just started getting to know. Somehow both sides of the woman fit like a glove.

When Ava's eyes found hers, she winked. Bianca's heart raced and her throat went dry with desire. Ava looked back down to the drums. Bianca blew out a long breath and threw back the rest of her beer. *Wow, this is going to be a very interesting six months, if it lasts that long.*

❖

After they left the Wet Whistle, Ava drove a few miles down the road. She pulled into the empty gravel parking lot at the public boat slip of the Stockbridge Bowl. As she parked close to the water, she indicated a bench off to one side. "Sit with me?"

"Of course," Bianca said.

Ava took a moment to take in the view of Lake Mahkeenac. The light of the nearly full moon bounced off its smooth surface. It was breathtaking. The gentle night breeze lifted Bianca's curly black hair, and she ached to touch it. She kept her hands to herself, knowing if she reached out now, she would lose control of the conversation she needed to have. She studied Bianca's beautiful profile. Her expression carefully blank. Over the years since she first met Bianca, Ava had imagined bringing her to this scenic spot more than once, but she never imagined figuring out what to say to her would be so difficult.

"So, *BJ*, why did you agree to write my biography?"

Bianca took a breath and a moment before answering. She turned to Ava and looked her in the eye. "Two years ago, I knew you were an extraordinary woman. From the moment we met, you were different from anyone I had ever encountered. You're kind and compassionate, a singular talent, strong and tender, gorgeous." Bianca blushed with that admission.

"Thank you," Ava said.

"I'm not finished. You found a way to comfort me in one of my darkest hours. You gave me the gift of you and your music. From that first day, I knew you were special. Everything I have learned about you since then has simply confirmed that fact for me."

When Ava opened her mouth again, Bianca stopped her by shaking her head slightly.

"There's more. When I was contacted about writing your biography, I'll admit I was scared at first. What if I dug into your life and found something that made the grand image vanish? What if what I saw and experienced two years ago was a wonderful illusion? But I couldn't stop wondering about who you were. I decided it was worth the risk. I wanted to get to know you better. Not only to write about your incredible life, but to know you. All of you...as deeply as you will let anybody see. That's all a good biographer can do, get to the 'you' that you will allow people to see and share that with the world."

"What if I told you I don't want you to write my biography?"

"Just me or anyone?"

"Anyone really. The biography was Hank's idea."

"I would say, okay. I'm disappointed because I believe your story is worth sharing, but the best biographies of living people are written in cooperation with the subject. If you don't want your story told, I'll tell Hank I won't do it. But I still want to get to know you for personal reasons, and I hope you're open to that. If not, I'll just have to admire you from afar and continue to listen to your music."

Ava studied Bianca's even gaze. "You could really do that? Walk away from the job? From me?"

Fierceness flashed briefly through Bianca's deep brown eyes. "Please don't misunderstand; walking away from you would not be a simple thing. But I like and respect you too much to try to change your mind if it's made up. But the job…there are other jobs. I would love to write your biography, almost as much as I want to get to know you. But if me walking out of your life is what would make you happiest, then all I'd ask is you take me home and you'll never have to see me again."

Ava watched the light sparkle off the lake while she pondered all Bianca had shared. The idea of never seeing Bianca again was not something Ava wanted to think about. Finally, she turned and took her hand. "Bianca, I want to get to know you too." Ava smiled as Bianca released a tremulous breath. "We had a connection when we first met. I still feel it. I want to explore that and spend time with you. The problem is, if you're not writing my biography, I'm afraid we won't get to spend much time together. I travel a lot and I'm not in this area very often."

Bianca gently squeezed Ava's hand. "So where does that leave us?"

"I don't know. What if you tagged along with us doing research for the biography? Then we could hang out, quite often in private, as much as we wanted. Hank did actually have some convincing reasons why I should get on board with the biography, but I'm not ready to say yes or no—just maybe."

"I have an idea," Bianca said.

"I'm listening."

"Let's compromise. I'll plan to accompany you for four or five weeks. You agree to let me write an article. Call it a test balloon if you like. You get an idea of what it would be like for me to gather information as though I was going to do the biography, because I'll still be working as though that is the end goal, but all you're committed to at this point is one article. Then, even if you ultimately decide not to go forward with the book, I still have something concrete I can produce from our time together."

"I think I could get behind that idea."

"You will have to decide one way or another at some point about the bigger story."

"I know. But in the meantime, I like this compromise. It gives me more time to consider things. But I do have one condition if we move forward," Ava said.

"Which is?"

"The time you and I spend together. It can't be a one-way street. I want to get to know you too. You have to answer as many questions and share as many stories about yourself as I do."

Bianca's smile lit her whole face. "I can live with that."

"Then it's a plan." Instead of extending her hand to seal the deal, she leaned over and gently touched her lips to Bianca's.

When they broke apart, Bianca met her gaze. "One more thing, I'd like to clear up. I owe you an apology for last time."

"You don't. I would have liked to get to know you back then, but I know you were overwhelmed with your grief and you needed time and space to heal. The timing was awful. Perhaps this time around, we can get to know one another," Ava said.

"I would like that a lot. But to be honest, I'm not sure how much I'm ready for."

"We'll take it slowly and keep it light and easy."

"Thank you."

CHAPTER THREE

The next morning, Bianca slipped quietly into the back of the music room in Tanglewood's Ozawa Hall. Hank had let her know Ava was holding a session for some of the young musicians in residence at the Tanglewood fellowship program. As soon as she heard about it, Bianca knew she wanted to see this side of Ava. The young adults studying violin sat in chairs formed in a half circle around her.

As Bianca sank into a seat in the back of the room, Ava looked up and their eyes met. Time slowed. Bianca felt the same connection she had several times before. With a look, Ava had the power to pull Bianca in. Sometimes she felt powerless to look away when their eyes locked. In those moments, Bianca felt like Ava could reach into her and know what she was feeling, even thinking. It was exhilarating but overwhelming. Every time their gaze broke Bianca felt vulnerable. And Ava, she would return to whatever it was she had been doing. Performing on stage, fighting with Hank, or working with students. It didn't seem to affect her at all.

When Ava returned her focus to her students, Bianca relaxed and observed her interactions with the young violinists. Ava wore a pair of hip-hugging forest green jeans, a sleeveless blouse a few shades lighter, and dark brown open-toed sandals. Her hair was pulled back into the ponytail making her appear young and carefree. The image she projected was relaxed yet professional, perfect given the setting. Bianca wondered briefly if Ava was dressed perfectly for every occasion. Ava seemed comfortable in every setting and situation. Bianca jotted down a note about that. Confidence? Carefree? How did she develop that skill? Was it trained or innate?

Each time she witnessed Ava on stage, she was awestruck by her abilities. Watching her now, giving careful guidance, help, and making minor adjustments to how one student held his violin, or how another needed to lift her chin ever so slightly, it was clear she was also a gifted instructor. Some of the students were obviously starstruck by Ava, given their reaction and rapt attention to her. She gave every one of them her time and consideration. Bianca knew firsthand how powerful Ava's attention was.

Ava lost her train of thought as she met Bianca's gaze again. She caught herself before she allowed her lustful thoughts to take over completely. Fortunately, when she looked back at the student she'd been addressing, he was still making slight adjustments to execute her critique. Still, the zing of attraction Ava always felt when she saw Bianca warmed her from the inside.

She had the student play for a few moments, so she could examine his technique. Part of her brain drifted to the seats in back. She probably should have expected Bianca to show up. Hank knew where she'd be. If she'd thought about it, she might have invited Bianca herself.

As the student finished playing, she gently adjusted his finger positions and asked him to play again. The other students looked on awaiting their turn for individual attention. As he began, his look of surprised pleasure made it clear he could hear the difference too. Ava enjoyed spending time with these teenagers and young adult students, sharing insights and helping them on their journey to become better musicians. Playing her violin for people was exceptional in its own way, but influencing the next generation of violinists at different venues around the globe…that held a special place in her heart. The summer music program at Tanglewood was probably her favorite because she loved the area so much, but she enjoyed working with passionate young people all over the world. Even when language was a barrier, music was not.

Several of the students stayed after the allotted time to ask more questions. Ava took all the time needed to answer each query in detail. Once the last student filed out, Ava spent a few moments putting away her violin and packing up her messenger bag. She glanced toward the back of the room and was pleasantly surprised to see Bianca still there, still watching her. She slung her bag over her shoulder, grabbed her violin case, and strode up the aisle toward her. "Hi."

"Hello. I hope you didn't mind I snuck in to watch," Bianca said.

"Not at all, I only wish I'd thought to invite you myself." They moved toward the exit and walked out into the bright sunshine.

"I enjoyed watching you interact with the students. You have a special way with them. I could tell even from back here that each of them felt seen and heard."

"Thank you. That's quite a compliment. It's fun for me."

"I could tell."

"I've been wanting to get over to the gardens on the other end of the property. Would you like to go for a walk?"

"I'd love to. Do you need to put your things in the car or something?"

"I never leave my violin in a vehicle. I'll carry it for now," Ava said.

"Okay. Since there are many gardens, I'll let you lead the way."

"It's not too far." Ava looked around them before she shifted her violin to her right hand so she could reach for Bianca's hand with her left.

"Worried someone will see us?"

"I'd rather Hank not know about us for now."

"I guess that makes sense, given our arrangement. Is he here today?"

"He shouldn't be, but these days I don't seem to know what he's up to. I mean, he did hire a biographer without my knowledge."

"There is that. So, the gardens…do you have a favorite flower?"

"Hibiscus, petunias, lilies…I love them all and I love trees. Really everything in nature. I try to spend as much time outside as I can, except when I have a chance to visit an art or science museum. I often spend time outside just sitting with my thoughts or getting lost in a great book. The first day I met you, I was headed to sit on the bench where I found you, just to breathe in the fresh air and soak in the beauty Tanglewood offers."

"Lucky me. There is a great view from that bench."

"It was even better that day."

"Right, because a distraught woman always enhances the view."

"Not any distraught woman necessarily, I wouldn't think. But you certainly improve any vista you're in."

"You're quite the charmer, Ava Wellington."

"Am I? I'm only speaking the truth." Once in the gardens, Ava steered them to a bench. "Would you mind sitting here for a bit?"

"I guess, sure. Why?"

Ava pulled her violin from its case. "I'd love to play a song for you, if that's all right."

"In that case, I'll sit here as long as you like. I love listening to you make beautiful music. For future reference, feel free to play for me, whenever you'd like."

Ava raised her violin to her chin and rested the instrument on her shoulder. She began to play. She wanted to play for Bianca. The fact that she'd never felt compelled to play for any other woman didn't have to mean anything. Did it? Finally, the music gripped her and she let go of conscious thought. She locked eyes with Bianca and played from the heart.

She felt the music pouring out of her. As though the instrument that was so much a part of her knew what she was trying to communicate. So much emotion, she had nowhere else to put it, except her violin. It's where she always released her deepest feelings. This was how she could let Bianca know how she felt, because she didn't have words yet.

Bianca sat motionless, captivated. She was so easily drawn into the music Ava played. She shivered with the intensity of the emotion Ava conveyed with her violin. Ava was playing solely for her and that increased the effect the music had on Bianca. Even with a warm breeze blowing, Bianca felt goose bumps form on her skin. She couldn't remember ever experiencing a more perfect musical moment. She shook her head to try to clear the haze. Her gaze dropped to Ava's long, slender fingers working her instrument.

It was easy to imagine those magical fingers running up and down her body. She closed her eyes to try to close off the sight flooding her senses, but that only enhanced the images in her mind. She swayed to the music flowing around her and allowed her throbbing center to gently hit the bench over and over again. It wouldn't quite bring her the release she craved, but it certainly didn't hurt.

She licked her suddenly dry lips and clenched her hands on her thighs. If she wasn't careful she'd forget herself and reach to quench the lovely ache between her legs. She opened her eyes to remind herself that she wasn't alone and someone else could come by at any moment and disrupt their magical moment. It didn't help to be confronted with the desire painted in bold strokes across the planes of Ava's face. Bianca couldn't be sure if Ava knew how much her playing impacted her, but she was clearly not unaffected herself.

As the last notes faded on the breeze, Bianca reined in her libido. If this was how she responded to Ava playing one song for her in the middle of the day, how would she survive watching her play night after night? Bianca clapped, genuinely happy to be exactly where she was. Ava lowered her violin and put it back in its case. "That was beautiful, Ava. Thank you for playing for me."

"I'm really glad you liked it, but it was my pleasure. Watching you as I play, I know you appreciate the music, very much."

Bianca wasn't sure what to make of Ava's words. Did she know how turned on she'd been or was she really only talking about her enjoyment of the music?

CHAPTER FOUR

Bianca stood looking out her back window. She was too preoccupied to actually appreciate the view of her gardens. She held the tour itinerary in her hand. She glanced down again at the list of cities she would be traveling to with Ava. Tomorrow they were headed for San Francisco. Then next week, they embarked upon the first leg of the European tour. Launching in Berlin, followed by Paris, London, Cologne, Hamburg, and Vienna, among others she couldn't place. She and Karen had not traveled overseas very much, but some of the places she might get to experience with Ava were places she had never even heard of let alone dreamed of going.

She put the itinerary in her bag and continued to check items off her list. She was almost done packing the necessities, but she wanted to pack a couple of books to read when there was down time. She wandered to her stacks of titles she had yet to read and selected three and added them to the suitcase.

Bianca knew it seemed like she'd jumped at the chance to write Ava's biography one way or another, but the truth was she was struggling with the idea. Some biographers might see this situation as questionable, and she had some reservations herself. But the compromise they'd reached was amicable either way. She knew she was already past the point of remaining neutral where Ava was concerned. In fact, she suspected their connection would lead them quickly into an intimate relationship.

In the end, she decided, it wasn't completely necessary to remain unattached. Many biographers in the past had gotten close with their subjects, maintaining lifelong friendships even after the book was published. This wasn't exactly the same thing, but Bianca decided not to give it too much weight at this point. She lost her wife two years ago and hadn't been intimate with anyone since then. Ava made her feel things, good things and Bianca was definitely ready to explore that.

She wouldn't deny Ava made her feel good, and she saw no harm in exploring those feelings. It wasn't even a predetermined outcome that she would, in fact, be writing Ava's biography. If Ava consented and agreed to the biography, she'd cross that bridge when she came to it.

There was no denying she was attracted to Ava. Even from their brief time together, it was obvious Ava found her attractive as well. The kisses they'd shared left no doubt about that. Maybe it was possible for her to simply have a fling. She definitely wouldn't say no to sexy time with Ava. Bianca fantasized about it, she felt herself flush hot thinking about it. *This could be fun.* That reminded her, she wanted to take some lingerie.

Bianca wouldn't delude herself into believing she wouldn't develop feelings for Ava. If she became intimate with her, it was bound to happen. That's the way she was wired. Hell, they'd barely spent more than twelve hours together and she was already quite fond of her. She would thoroughly enjoy the time they had and treasure the memories they created. At least that is what she hoped she'd be able to do. Vigilance was the name of the game. She needed to remain alert for any sign she was getting too clingy or becoming too attached. Ava would be turned off by that she was sure, so she'd have to be on the lookout for that behavior in herself and nip it in the bud if it cropped up.

Part of her couldn't believe she and Ava had worked out a compromise that would allow them both to feel good about Bianca joining the tour. Still, Bianca couldn't bring herself to look beyond the next four or five weeks of the schedule. That's what they'd agreed to, and if Ava remained opposed to having her biography written after that time, Bianca knew they would need to reassess the bounds of their relationship. *Relationship? Wow, you're already thinking relationship.*

❖

A part of Ava was thrilled at the prospect of spending quality time with Bianca. The other parts of her were utterly terrified. The part of her that was excited had her pacing endlessly in her hotel room, trying to work off her anxiousness before seeing her again. Nobody had ever affected her as Bianca had. Ava certainly hadn't been a saint the last two years, but she no longer found her one-night stands as exciting as she once had. She longed for something more…substantial, real, and meaningful. She was tired of having sex without any emotion or connection.

Maybe tired wasn't quite right. But these days, more often than not, she preferred to go back to her hotel room alone rather than leave another woman's room or home after a night of abandon. Whenever she resorted to that recently, she felt lonelier afterward. It didn't seem worth it anymore. Ava was changing; she just didn't know exactly what that meant for a woman who lived her life on tour. She craved something deeper, but relationships had never really worked for her. Maybe it was time to try again. This time with someone she hadn't stopped thinking about for two years.

Ava knew she was walking a fine line. She didn't want her biography written. She didn't want the biggest secret of her life being discovered and divulged. She wasn't even worried about herself much, but she didn't want that secret to hurt those she loved most. She couldn't think of any other way Bianca would have agreed to come on tour with her. So she consented to hold off on making a final decision about the book, but agreed to an article. She had four or five weeks to figure it out. But what if she couldn't?

She was grateful when a soft knock on her hotel room door saved her from going down that path again. "Yes?"

"Hey, it's Vicki."

Ava opened the door for her assistant. "Is it that time already?"

"Yes, I just need your bags. Then we can swing by and pick up Bianca on the way to the airport."

The idea of seeing Bianca again had Ava's skin humming with excitement. "Great, let's go."

Vicki looked at Ava in surprise. "I thought you didn't want your life story told."

"I don't," Ava said without thinking it through.

Vicki winked and gave her a knowing smile. "Then I'll just keep how excited you are about seeing your biographer quiet."

Ava blew out a hard breath and met Vicki's gaze. "Thanks."

"Of course." Vicki picked up Ava's bags and headed for the Suburban hired to take them to Boston Logan Airport.

Bianca stepped out into the sunshine and stood on the porch. Ava's mouth went dry with desire. She hopped out of the truck and bounded up the stairs before the driver could grab the bags. She didn't reach for them. Instead she stood in front of Bianca. "Is this everything?" Ava indicated the garment bag, suitcase, and laptop bag.

"Yes. I only packed for four weeks. If I end up staying beyond that, I'll need to find a laundry."

Ava breathed a sigh of relief. At least Bianca wasn't giving up yet. "Ah, okay. You have your passport?"

"I do." Bianca stepped to Ava and put her hand on her arm. "Why are you so nervous?"

Ava stared for a moment at the hand that centered her. Then she looked into Bianca's eyes. "This feels like a really big deal. I don't want to mess it up."

"Just be yourself and we'll be fine."

Ava wished she could be so sure. "We should go. It will take at least three hours to get to the airport."

After everyone was settled in the Suburban, the driver headed toward Boston. Vicki sat in front, giving Ava and Bianca the roomy back seat.

Bianca turned toward Ava getting comfortable in the seat. "How about we use this time for an informal interview, so you can get comfortable with some of the types of questions I'll be asking you over the next few weeks or months?"

"Um, okay, but remember our deal; I get to ask questions too."

"I remember." Bianca studied Ava's vibrant blue eyes and wondered again what it was about the idea of having her life story told that could make this successful, confident, woman so uncomfortable. This was such a stark contrast to every other situation she'd seen her in. There was something going on. "Let's start with an easy one. Where were you born?"

The corners of Ava's mouth lifted into the barest hint of a smile. "St. Petersburg, Russia."

"What? Really?"

Ava chuckled. "Not as simple as you thought, is it?"

Bianca recovered quickly. She wondered what else she would learn about Ava during their time together. She was looking forward to the discovery. "Obviously, there is more that I need to learn about you than I thought. Please continue."

Ava nodded slightly. "I was born Katarina Alkaev. From what I've been told, my birth mother died during childbirth, and no father was listed on the birth certificate. The Wellingtons adopted me and I went to live with them in London when I was eight days old. They are all I've ever known. Here's a fun fact, Alkaev means 'wished for,' and because I was, Mum and Dad kept that as my middle name."

"I had no idea."

"Very few people do," Ava said matter-of-factly.

"So, you grew up in London?"

"For the most part, yes, in the southwestern part of London. It was a good childhood. My parents were always open with me about where I came from, and I knew how much I was wanted."

"That's certainly more than some people can say. Do you have any siblings?"

Ava stared out the side window so long, apparently lost in thought, Bianca started to think she wasn't going to answer. When she finally did, her voice was low. "My parents adopted Lara when I was sixteen."

Was that hard for you? Did you feel replaced? Those were the questions she wanted to ask, but it felt too soon. Instead she asked the most obvious question. "You have a sister?" In her preliminary research, Bianca hadn't uncovered that. She wondered if keeping her family life so private was her nature or a necessity of her fame.

Ava didn't say anything more.

"Are you close?"

"Not especially. With the age difference, my going to school abroad, and then my travel schedule, there was never a lot of time to really develop a deep bond."

There was no emotion in her voice, as though she'd prepared the answer and was simply reading from some hidden script. Almost like she was talking about a stranger. Her voice was flat. It was clear she did not want to elaborate further. In fact, Bianca got the sense Ava had no desire to talk about her sister at all. She wondered why. Ava had disengaged as quickly as she'd begun. Bianca made a note to return to this later.

Bianca knew at some point they would need to delve deeper, but she saw no reason to push so early. She decided to take the conversation in a different direction. "When did music become a part of your life?"

Ava visibly relaxed with the question. "Very early on, my mum had me taking piano lessons soon after I could climb up on the bench by myself. She found me playing with the keys one day. Apparently, I wasn't pounding them like a lot of kids would. I was just pushing them down one at a time to listen to the sound each one made. The way she tells the story, I was delighted by the sound of each note. Soon afterward, she decided to find me a teacher and see where things went."

"How old were you?" Bianca asked.

"Three. I was barely speaking full sentences yet. For my fourth birthday, my parents took me to a concert at the London Symphony Orchestra. The two major things I remember about that night are the fancy dress I got to wear and the solo violinist. I loved all the music, but when the soloist came onstage and played, I was mesmerized. I played those songs over in my head for days."

"I can imagine you in your fancy dress completely taken with the music."

"I was. I begged my parents for a violin after that. One day my father came home with a one-sixteenth-sized violin for me. I loved it. I transitioned to violin lessons and never looked back." Ava grinned at Bianca. "Now, that's enough about me. Where were you born?"

"San Ysidro, California. My mom and dad came up from Mexico for the wedding of one of my mom's cousins. She was only eight months pregnant at the time, but with the travel and the excitement of the wedding, she went into premature labor and had me at the hospital in San Ysidro."

"Any siblings?"

"Four sisters and a brother. In fact, my sister Elena lives in San Francisco."

"You have a sister in San Francisco? Are you going to see her while we're there this week?"

"I'm going to try. But with her schedule and me working on the book, I didn't know if I'd have time."

"You have to. You can't go all that way and not see your sister."

Ava's intensity surprised Bianca given her lackluster response to questions about her own sister. But she wasn't going to argue if it meant seeing Elena. "Okay, I'll figure out a way to make it happen."

"You could invite her to a show. I'll leave a ticket for her. Then you two could have dinner afterward."

"You don't have to do that. She's my sister; I'll figure it out."

Ava touched Bianca's arm. "I'd like to, that is if you think she'd enjoy it."

Bianca covered Ava's hand with hers, wanting to maintain the contact a moment longer. "I'm sure she would. Thank you."

"You're welcome."

"What was life like for you growing up as an only child? Because that's essentially what you were for most of your childhood, right?" Bianca asked.

Ava took a moment to think before she spoke. "True. I don't remember much before I was four or five, but it seems like the feeling of love and being wanted was always there when I was little. My mum was home all the time, and she played with me a lot even though I always had a nanny. We also had a housekeeper and a cook, so I guess my mum had the time to spend with me. I never thought anything of it until I left home. I mean everyone around me seemed to have the same things. It wasn't until I got out into the world on my own that I realized how much privilege I had. Still have."

"Tell me something about your childhood that not a lot of people know," Bianca said.

Ava was quiet for several moments, perhaps trying to think of something that wasn't so private. Finally, she smiled. "Whenever me and my mum would go out on walks when I was little, she'd encourage me to touch the bushes, leaves, shrubs, flowers, and trees to feel the different textures and recognize or name the various colors. We would stop and watch ants march in straight lines and spiders spin intricate webs. We'd pick up rocks and watch birds take flight. My mum once told me she started the practice while I was still in the pram. I'm sure taking that time with each aspect of nature taught me to appreciate all the variations large and small in the world around me."

"I imagine that's why you love nature and being outside so much."

"I believe it is. I'll always be grateful to my mum for giving me those opportunities and experiences."

Bianca could almost imagine a little Ava so curious about the world. It made her wonder what that experience would be like.

"What made you sad just now?" Ava asked.

"Your story made me think about children. Specifically, what it would have been like to have had a little girl."

"I'm sorry. You know you could still have that someday."

"Maybe." Bianca didn't want to dwell on the past or think about an uncertain future right now. "Have you ever thought about having kids?" Bianca asked.

"Um." Ava paused. "Sure I've thought about it. But with my travel schedule it's not very realistic. Ava looked out the window. "Oh wow, I didn't realize we were already so close to the airport. Talking with you certainly makes time fly."

The abrupt change in Ava threw Bianca for a minute. She made a mental note to ask this question again when they wouldn't be interrupted.

CHAPTER FIVE

Under Vicki's watchful eye, all the bags were unloaded onto a flat cart. Bianca held onto her laptop bag and Ava carried her violin. They made their way inside, and Vicki led the way to the line for the first class check-in.

Bianca stopped short and Ava barely avoided running into her. "What's wrong?" Ava asked.

"I've never flown first class. It's not necessary. I can fly coach no problem."

"It's one of the perks of the job. Besides, this way we can sit next to each other on the flight."

"Well, when you put it like that…"

"Come on, it'll be fine."

Bianca relented and followed Ava and Vicki as they all checked in and then through security. Her next surprise came when Vicki led them to one of the lounges for first class passengers. She'd heard about them but never been inside one. But she was confused by the sign on the door. "I don't understand how we can go in here when we're not flying on this airline."

Vicki held up three similar looking black cards. "These priority passes get us into most of the lounges in all the different airports we travel between. Ava prefers I carry hers. Would you like me to keep yours or would you like to hold on to it?"

"Uh, I guess I'll keep it. Thank you."

Vicki handed all three cards to the young man behind the counter. He scanned them and handed them back. She gave one to Bianca. Bianca felt the cold, hard plastic between her fingers and slipped the card into the side pocket of her bag. Shortly after the three of them were settled into seats, Bianca felt Ava stiffen next to her. She glanced up and then looked to where Ava's gaze was fixed. Hank and Steven were walking toward them. Their styles could not have been more different. Hank was in a full three-piece suit, his tie tightly knotted. Steven wore a skintight salmon tank covered by an open button-down collared shirt with the sleeves rolled up, khaki slacks, and boat shoes.

Ava announced, "I need a drink." She stood and walked away.

Hank followed her while Steven dropped into her vacant seat and whispered to Bianca, "Don't go to her right now. The two of them need to work this out on their own. I get the feeling that for some reason Ava doesn't want Hank to know about the understanding you've come to."

"She told you about our agreement?"

"Yes, she tells me almost everything."

"Maybe it should be you I'm interviewing."

Steven shook his head. "You're likely to get much less out of me than you are her. That's why she trusts me." His eyes twinkled. It was clear Ava's secrets were safe with him.

Bianca understood the close bond of siblings, and even though Ava and Steven weren't related, she imagined their relationship was similar to what she had with her sisters and brother, so she didn't bristle at the subtle warning. Instead she met Steven's protectively fierce gaze squarely. "I won't ever ask you to betray her confidence."

"Then you and I shouldn't have any problem."

Bianca blew out an exaggerated breath. "Thank goodness, because no matter how much she likes me, I get the feeling if her mama bear had problems with me, it would be a very difficult decision."

Steven laughed loudly. "I don't think either one of us want to find out who would win that one."

Ava reclaimed her seat next to Bianca almost as soon as Steven left. "What was that all about?"

"We were just putting our cards on the table."

"I see. Anything I should be worried about?"

"Nothing at all. He's just looking out for you. I understand and appreciate anyone who wants to do that."

"Okay."

"I've been wondering, will we always travel on Tuesday?"

"Monday or Tuesday, depending on whether I have a lesson scheduled with students on Monday. If we travel Monday, Tuesday will be a free day. Every so often, if the Sunday show is early and there is no lesson the next day, we'll travel Sunday night so we have both Monday and Tuesday free."

"In general, will every week be similar?" Bianca asked.

"Basically, most places the shows are Wednesday, Friday, and Saturday evenings, and Sundays either late afternoon or evening, depending on the location. Sometimes there won't be a Wednesday show. Mondays are when I do the lessons for every place that has a fellowship program or other music program like Tanglewood. Also, we'll spend two weeks in London. That's built into the schedule every time we're there so I can spend a little time with my family."

"That must be nice." Bianca wondered if she'd get to meet Ava's family. It would certainly help to get that history and witness those dynamics if she was going to do a biography, but it wasn't really needed for the article.

"It is. I can ask Vicki to get you a more detailed schedule if you'd like. She already has it in her calendar."

"That would be nice. Thank you. I imagine you'll have rehearsals with the different groups?"

"Yes, those are generally several hours long on Wednesday, whether there is a show that night or not. Those can be pretty long days. On the plus side, Thursday is always off, so we can sleep in."

"Good to know. Will I be able to interview the students and other musicians, especially the ones you've worked with before?"

"Do you need to?"

"Yes, it would be helpful."

"I'm sure we can figure something out. It's almost time to board. Are you ready?" Ava asked.

There was a time in Bianca's life when flying had been exciting and fun. It had been no problem for her when she'd flown across country from California to go to school in Amherst, Massachusetts. She and Karen had flown back numerous times to visit her family, and they'd traveled to Europe a couple times. Bianca never had any issues with the plane rides. But for the last two years, since Karen died, the thought of getting in a plane wracked Bianca with anxiety. Up until now, she'd managed to avoid it. Her family had all come to her for Karen's funeral, and when she went to see them she'd opted for the longer train ride.

She had known this time would come eventually, but so far she had managed to put it from her thoughts for the most part. She'd managed to push the fears to the side. But now, the time had come. If she was going to travel with Ava, she would have to get on that plane.

There was no way to avoid it now, and the dread paralyzed her. She stared off into the distance, unable to tear her gaze away from the images playing through her mind of all the disasters that could happen during a flight. Her heart raced and white noise shut her ears to all the activity happening around her. Suddenly, the fog started to lift and she felt calmness settle over her. From far away she heard, "Bianca…Bianca look at me."

She fought to focus. Ava knelt in front of her, her hands gripping Bianca's upper arms. Ava was all she could see. She took in the features of her beautiful face and the concern etched on it.

"Bianca, are you okay?"

Bianca nodded slightly, surprised that she almost meant it. Ava's touch kept her focus in the present, not on all the things that might happen. "Yeah, sorry, I just need another minute."

When Ava started to release her, Bianca pleaded, "Please don't let go of me. You're the only thing keeping me from a full-blown panic attack right now."

Ava slid her hands down Bianca's arms and clasped her hands. "What's going on?"

Before Bianca answered, she became aware enough of her surroundings to realize they had quite the audience. Steve, Vicki, and Hank looked on with concern. When Ava realized what Bianca was looking at, she took action. "How about the three of you board? Vicki, would you please take my case? Bianca and I will be right behind you."

Each of them looked relieved to have something concrete to do. Once they were gone, Ava refocused on Bianca.

"What happened just now?"

"I think it's pretty safe to say I had a panic attack."

"I got that, but why?"

"I haven't been able to get on a plane since Karen died."

"Oh my God, Bianca, why didn't you say something?"

"I have to be able to get on a plane to keep up with you and your travel schedule."

"You know I don't care about that. I do care about you."

Bianca appreciated the sentiment, but she couldn't focus on that right now. "I care about doing a good job, and I can't do that from Massachusetts while you travel all over the world. I want to do this. I knew what I was signing up for. I need to do this."

"Okay, then let's do it together."

Ava and Bianca were nearly the last to board the plane, but they did make it on. Bianca wouldn't let go of Ava's hand, and that was fine with Ava. She couldn't forget the look of sheer terror on Bianca's face a short time ago. She wanted to protect her from that pain. Once they were seated and buckled in, Ava asked the flight attendant for two gin and tonics. When the drinks were placed in front of her she handed one to Bianca. "Here, drink this."

Bianca quickly consumed the first drink.

Ava swapped the empty glass for the still full one. "Sip this one."

Bianca took a sip and set the glass on her own tray before looking at Ava. "Thank you for taking care of me."

"You're welcome." *It's all I ever wanted to do.*

As the flight attendants made final preparations for takeoff, Ava looked at Bianca. "Tell me about your sister Elena. You said she was in law school, right?"

Later, when Bianca had time to think about it, she realized the distraction Ava created kept her from being fully aware of taxiing and takeoff. She added that to her growing list of reasons to be grateful to Ava. They were underway. Time would tell how many weeks they would spend together. But Bianca was excited by the possibilities ahead of them.

Ava made so many things possible. After Karen died in a plane crash, Bianca wasn't sure she'd ever be able to fly again. She'd taken this job knowing how much travel was involved. It had lingered in the back of her mind since she'd signed onto the project. But, the idea of getting to spend time with Ava always outweighed her fears. At least until she had to get on the plane.

Ava had helped her through that though. Bianca wondered how she was able to distract her. The simple touch of Ava's hand seemed to ground her, calm her, and in the right moments, excite her. She knew getting on a plane wouldn't be easy, at least for a while, but in this moment, she knew if Ava was by her side, she would be able to do it. For the first time she knew she really could travel on the tour. *Thank you, Ava.*

❖

Bianca found she very much appreciated not having to oversee all the travel details. Vicki took care of everything. All she had to do was show up and keep up. As the group walked into the Fairmont Hotel atop Nob Hill, Bianca stopped to take in the grand details of the lobby. The expansive and opulent entrance and lobby were beautiful.

When Bianca had visited the city in the past, she'd never made it inside this building. It was out of her price range. This was all too much, a little dream like. She didn't plan to get used to it. She would say something to Ava when she had a chance. She didn't need to stay in any place so fancy. She'd also talk to Vicki. Vicki was Ava's assistant, not hers, and Bianca was perfectly capable of handling her own affairs. But since Vicki had all the information and she didn't, it was easier for now.

While Vicki dealt with hotel check-in, Ava pulled Bianca as "There's nothing on the agenda for tonight. I'd like to have din with you, just the two of us."

Bianca was fully aware of both the nervousness and the des, in Ava's eyes. "I would enjoy that. I don't have plans to see my sist until tomorrow since she has class tonight."

Ava's smile lit her whole face. "Lovely, I'll stop by your roor, at six."

"I'm looking forward to it. Ava, I wanted to talk to you about something else."

"Sure. What is it?"

"I don't need to stay at such an expensive hotel. I'm perfectly happy to stay somewhere more reasonable."

The corners of Ava's mouth turned down into a small frown. "I certainly don't want you to be uncomfortable. But I do like having you close. Everyone on the team stays at the same hotel as a matter of convenience for Vicki, so she can book the rooms more efficiently. I don't want you to worry about the expense of any of the places we'll stay. It's just a part of the deal."

Bianca breathed out a sigh. What Ava said made sense. She'd learn to go with it, maybe in time. "Okay, if you're sure."

"No question about it. You're where I want you too, so it's good for me and easy for Vicki."

Vicki approached them, and the bellhops stood at the ready with their bags. Vicki said, "You two are on the same floor. I'll take you up and make sure you have everything you need."

Bianca followed silently. She wasn't used to being waited on so attentively. But since everyone was headed in the same direction, there was no point in objecting.

She certainly didn't fault Ava for having an assistant. It made sense that someone could handle all those details for her so she could focus on her music. But once Bianca was done with the story, sooner if Ava wouldn't let her write it, she'd go back to Stockbridge and be on her own again.

The entire party stopped at the end of the hall. Vicki held out an envelope to Bianca and indicated the room on the left. "Bianca, this is your room."

Bianca used the key card to push her way into the room, a bellhop close on her heels. She got caught up looking out the wall of windows at the stunning view. By the time she turned, Vicki was tipping the bellhop. Once he left, Bianca stopped her. "Vicki, I could have done that. You don't need to take care of every little thing for me. I'm working, too."

Vicki smiled kindly. "It's my job."

"No, you're Ava's assistant."

"Right, and she asked me to handle all the details for you just as I do for her."

"I appreciate it and you're really good at your job, but it's not necessary."

"It's what the boss wants and she gets what she wants. You'll have to take it up with her."

"Thank you for everything."

"You're welcome."

Ava turned from the window as Vicki let herself into the room with the spare key. "Is Bianca all settled in?"

"She's getting there. She's uncomfortable with me handling all the details."

"Is it a problem for you?"

"Of course not, it's not much more work than I'm already doing."

"I'll talk to her. I do appreciate it and all that you do. I want her to be able to focus on why she's here and enjoy her time."

Vicki grinned. It was clear she understood what Ava wasn't saying as much as what she had.

Ava turned back to the window before asking, "The reservations are all set for tonight?"

"Yes, dinner for two at seven at Gary Danko. The special arrangements you requested will be accommodated. The car will be downstairs waiting for you at six so you have a bit of time to wander around the city if you want."

"Thank you."

"You're welcome."

Once Vicki left, Ava considered walking across the hall to chat with Bianca, but she didn't want to disturb her if she was resting. Instead, she sent her a quick text letting her know where they'd be having dinner. Then she took out her laptop and plugged in her headphones. She was feeling very inspired lately. She planned to spend the next few hours working on her latest composition. Hopefully, that would help her pass the time so she didn't wear a hole in the carpet pacing, waiting to take Bianca on a real date.

CHAPTER SIX

At precisely six, Ava closed her hotel room door and took the four steps across the hallway. She took a deep breath and rapped her knuckles sharply on Bianca's door. Bianca opened it. Ava took in all of Bianca in a simple but elegant red dress. Her luminous black curls cascaded over her shoulders. Her makeup expertly applied it almost appeared she had none on. "Wow. You are gorgeous," Ava said.

"Thank you. After you told me where we were going I looked it up and saw how fancy it is. How did you manage to get a reservation? It looks like they book months in advance."

"I have a few tricks up my sleeve, or I should say Vicki does, and I wanted to spoil you a little."

"I hope you know I don't need to be spoiled. But since the food looks so good, I'll let you this time."

"Fair enough. The car is waiting downstairs. Shall we?"

Bianca wrapped her arm around Ava's outstretched arm. "Absolutely."

"We have a little extra time before dinner. Would you like to do a little sightseeing?"

"Sure, but I wouldn't mind doing some after dinner as well."

Ava couldn't decide from Bianca's tone if she was talking about seeing San Francisco or something more intimate. She decided to err on the side of caution. "We can certainly do that. We have the car as long as we want it this evening. I did ask the driver to take us down Lombard Street on the way."

"I'd love to see it again. Do you have places you like to revisit in all the cities you tour?"

"Most of them and I'm looking forward to sharing them with you," Ava said, hoping she wasn't giving away too much.

"I can't wait."

As the driver slowly navigated the hairpin turns of Lombard Street, Bianca turned from the window to find Ava watching her intently. She slid closer to her. "Are you okay?"

"I'm wonderful." Ava laid her hand on Bianca's leg.

"What are you thinking about?" Bianca asked as she linked her fingers with Ava's.

"You."

"What about me?"

"I was just thinking about how much I'm enjoying spending time with you."

"The feeling is mutual."

"I'm glad. Is there anything you'd like to see this evening?"

"No, I'm along for the ride, willing to go wherever you'd like to show me."

"I thought perhaps we could drive down the Embarcadero and explore a bit of Fisherman's Wharf before dinner."

"That sounds lovely."

Ava reached for Bianca's hand as they got out of the car and kept hold of it as they walked into the restaurant. They were shown to their table immediately. Once their drinks arrived, Bianca raised her glass. "Here's to new experiences and to getting to know one another better."

"Cheers." Ava set her drink down and leaned forward. "Can I ask you something personal?"

"Yes."

"What's your biggest regret in life?"

"Oh my, nothing like starting with an easy one."

"You can choose not to answer, but I really want to get to know you. I figure if we start with some of the harder stuff, the rest will come more quickly."

"Fair enough. But I hope you're ready for this."

"Come on, then."

"I'd have to say my biggest regret in life is that I'll never get to know my daughter."

Ava laid her hand on Bianca's on top of the table. *She still misses her unborn daughter. There is no way I can tell her about Lara. She would hate me if she knew I gave up my daughter when she'll never have the chance to meet hers.* "I'm so sorry." It didn't feel like enough, but Ava didn't know what else to say.

"Yeah, me too. I would have loved raising a little girl. Like you said earlier, maybe it will still happen one day. Anyway, perhaps we can talk about something else. We got interrupted when I asked this question earlier. Have you ever thought about having kids?"

Ava took a sip to buy time to formulate her answer. "I have a lot actually. But with all the travel I do, it doesn't seem fair to raise children in this environment."

"I don't know. I think children can cope with a lot if they know they're loved and you'll always be there for them. But that brings up another interesting question. Have you ever considered when or if you'll stop touring?"

"I've been thinking about that quite a bit lately. You're the first person I've said this to, so please keep it quiet. I've considered starting a production/training company where I would train up-and-coming musicians. I would also like to have studio space so I could record their music. I don't have everything figured out just yet, but it's an idea I've been rolling around for a while now. I know I don't want to keep up the crazy touring schedule forever, and I would get bored if I wasn't doing something productive."

"That sounds like a very ambitious project. I have no doubt you will excel in that realm as well.

"Thank you. That means a lot."

"Have you given any thought to where you might want to locate the school?"

"I haven't gotten as far as a locale. There are so many places I love. How about you? Have you ever considered writing something other than biographies? Or doing something completely different?"

"I have a few ideas for romance novels," Bianca said.

"Really? Why haven't you written them?" *How does she keep getting better the more I know her?*

"I guess for a long time, I didn't see them as 'real' writing. But I've discovered some fascinating lesbian fiction recently that has me reconsidering my views."

"I think romance gets a bad rap."

"Are you a fan?"

"You could say that. I'd read anything you write."

"I'll remember that." Bianca smiled over the rim of her glass as she sipped her cocktail.

Ava liked being the one to inspire that smile. She wanted to make it happen as often as possible. "In fact, I've downloaded all your books to my tablet. So far, I've not only read the Etheridge book, I also read the biography you wrote on Sandra Cisneros."

"You did not. Not many people even know about that book, I'm afraid."

"I did. I hadn't realized you do historical biographies as well."

"I don't usually. That was a passion project. I love her writing and wanted to find out more about her."

"It was really good. Your writing is so captivating. You made me want to know who she was. What inspired her? I'd never even heard of her before."

"Thank you. When I wrote it, I had a hard time deciding between her as my subject or Dolores Huerta. One day I'll probably tackle a book about Dolores as well."

"Well, you can count on me to read that one too," Ava said.

As the waitress placed their dinners in front of them, Bianca took a moment to reflect on what she'd shared about Karen and their daughter. She could have come up with something less personal to share, but she knew that wouldn't be authentic, and no matter what happened with her and Ava in the future, it was important to her that she be genuine too. Honesty and transparency would help build trust between them, and that was a good foundation for every relationship regardless of where this went. Bianca had mourned Karen and their unborn child. Tonight was not about them. This evening was about spending time with Ava, getting to know her better.

She wouldn't have hesitated if Ava wanted to go directly back to the hotel room and spend some more intimate time together. On one hand, she knew that was moving fast. On the other, it felt like they had known each other for a long time and it seemed they were headed that way. She was on the verge of suggesting they go back to her room when Ava spoke. "Would you like to go for cocktails at Top of the Mark?"

"Ooh, my sister told me about that place, but I've never been. It would be fun to see it."

"I'll just take care of the check and we can get out of here."

As they walked out of the restaurant, Bianca turned to Ava. "Thank you for dinner. It was incredible."

"You're welcome." Ava reached for Bianca's hand and they walked to the waiting car together. "Speaking of your sister, are you excited to see her tomorrow?"

"I am, very much."

"Good. Are you two close?"

"I have a good relationship with all my siblings, but I'm definitely closest with Elena. We're not closest in age, but we have similar mindsets about most things. It may also have something to do with both of us being lesbians."

"Oh I didn't realize. That's interesting. How do your parents do with that?"

"I've never felt anything besides support and love from them. I prepared for more resistance than I got when I came out to them given the Catholic thing. I don't know exactly what they thought, but they made me feel safe and loved and like my revelation wasn't going to change anything between us and it didn't."

"That's great."

"It really was. Then, Karen and I were already together before Elena ever voiced a preference one way or another, so it was quite a non-event for her. She didn't have to come out so much as confirm what most of us already suspected."

"Lucky her."

"Right? You'd think so. Sometimes she jokes that I stole all her thunder by coming out so many years before her."

"She sounds like quite a character."

"Oh, she is."

"I hope you have a wonderful time with her tomorrow. It looks like we're here." Once the car stopped at the curb, Ava got out and offered her hand to Bianca.

Bianca stepped out of the car and linked her arm with Ava's. She leaned into her as they crossed the lobby. She felt like she couldn't get close enough. She ran her fingernail slowly up and down the inside of Ava's arm, just above her wrist. The delicious shiver that ran through Ava delighted Bianca.

They were alone in the elevator. As the doors closed, Bianca turned to Ava and gently pulled her down for a kiss. She meant for it to be a sweet, simple kiss. But as soon as their lips connected, her body responded quickly. Her nipples hardened, her heart raced, and her clit throbbed.

Bianca wanted more. She needed more. She moved her hands from Ava's neck down her back to grip her tight butt. She pulled Ava closer. There were too many clothes between them. Bianca wanted Ava under her, over her, it didn't matter. She wanted her naked. The ding of the elevator brought her back to reality. She stepped back from Ava. They both struggled to catch their breath as the elevator doors slid open.

"Wow," Ava said softly.

Bianca grabbed her hand and chuckled. "You can say that again." As they walked through the door of the bar, Bianca was stunned by the dramatic views. The sun was just about to set over the Golden Gate Bridge. "Wow," Bianca said.

Ava laughed freely. "Exactly."

They were greeted and shown to a table near the windows.

When the waiter arrived, Ava ordered a drink for them both while Bianca tried in earnest to take in all she could see. The buildings in the skyline were brightly lit as the evening darkened around them. As she stared at the night sky, she thought about Ava sitting next to her. The entire evening with her had been so comfortable. No awkward silences even when they were covering heavy topics. For the most part Ava was open and seemed genuine in what she had to say. The more she got to know Ava, the more she liked her. Ava gave herself completely when they were intimate. Bianca only wished she could figure out why there were other times when it felt like Ava was holding back.

"I'm sorry what did you say?" Bianca glanced over at Ava who had pulled her from her deep thoughts.

"I asked if you're okay. You seemed really far away."

"I'm good. I was actually thinking about you."

"Oh?"

"Yes, I was thinking about how much I've enjoyed this evening and how much pleasure I'm finding in getting to know you."

"I feel the same." Ava stood and held out her hand. "Would you dance with me?"

"I'd love to."

Ava led Bianca to the dance floor. As their bodies met and they began dancing, Ava simply let herself feel. She felt the texture of Bianca's dress under her hand, their bodies pressed together, and Bianca's silky hair against her cheek as they danced closely. Dancing with Bianca, being this close to her in a room full of people where she had to keep some modicum of decorum, was exquisite torture.

She raised her head to gauge Bianca's reaction to their closeness and found the same raw desire. In that moment, there was nothing that could have stopped her from kissing Bianca. Her entire being focused on that one thing, and the only thing she wanted right then was to explore Bianca's lips again. She moved toward her, zeroed in, closed her eyes, and was surprised when her lips met Bianca's cheek instead of her lips.

Her eyes popped open and Ava tried to process what just happened. That's when she realized there was a woman standing next to them and the music had stopped. She looked between Bianca and the woman, trying to put the pieces together.

Then the woman spoke, looking directly at Ava. "I'm so sorry to disturb you, truly I am. But aren't you Ava Wellington?"

Ava cringed that someone had recognized her and ruined such an intimate moment with Bianca. It was unsettling. It wasn't that she minded being seen with Bianca; she was only disappointed that their time together had been interrupted. Regaining her composure, she finally took a couple steps back from Bianca, after shooting her a quick look of regret. "Yes, I am."

"I'm such a huge fan," the woman said.

"Thank you, that's always nice to hear. What's your name?" Ava would have laughed at how automatic the response was if she wasn't still throbbing for Bianca.

"I'm Barb. Now that I've already crashed your date, I wonder if I could ask a huge favor."

"What did you have in mind?"

"I'm part of the trio playing the music tonight. We're usually a quartet, but our second violinist is sick tonight. But I have her violin with me. It's certainly not as good as what you regularly play, but would you possibly like to join us for a song or two?"

Ava had only been vaguely aware of the trio playing soft, classical music before they walked to the dance floor. When they'd approach them though, almost as automatic as breathing, she noticed their individual techniques on their instruments. They clearly had some formal training. Ava looked back to Bianca who seemed unfazed but not unhappy. She met her gaze and raised her eyebrow in question.

"Go ahead, if you'd like," Bianca said.

Ava turned to Barb. "Okay. Give me a minute and I'll join you."

"Oh this is awesome. Thank you so much."

Ava took Bianca's hand and walked her back to their table. "Are you sure you're okay with this?"

"I'm absolutely sure. I love seeing you play," Bianca said.

"All right. To be clear though, I would like a chance to make up for the interruption later."

"I'm happy to have you do that as well," Bianca said.

"Lovely." Ava kissed Bianca on the cheek and went to join the trio.

Fame wasn't something Ava thought about often. She rarely focused on how well known she was in symphony and orchestral circles, never mind outside of them. Sometimes it amazed her that she was known outside that close-knit community. People probably wouldn't know her at all if she hadn't been asked to appear on some of the afternoon and late night talk shows.

She loved sharing her music with anyone who wanted to hear it, and it didn't matter to her that she was sometimes sandwiched between a teen actor or mega sports star and silly pet tricks. People connected with her music when they heard it and that was the important part. The music was everything. She had recorded more than two dozen albums, hoping to get her music out into the world, even when she couldn't be there to play it in person.

As famous as she was, even her biggest fans didn't usually recognize her when she wasn't dressed in the fashionable outfits and stage makeup she wore for the shows. When she took the fancy clothes off, wore muted makeup or none at all, and pulled her hair back, she could move in the world without being recognized. It was the best of all possible scenarios. It allowed her to travel pretty freely without being stopped frequently for pictures and autographs. Every so often, someone would look at her sideways as though they were trying to figure out why she looked familiar, but as long as she kept moving she was seldom disturbed.

She never minded signing autographs when someone did recognize her. Even more, she enjoyed spending a few minutes talking about the music. What their favorite piece was, if they had one, which shows they had been to, Ava was comfortable around people when she could focus on the music.

There was a trapping of her fame that Ava appreciated above all else. Being able to bring her team with her was essential for her. It made the road feel a bit less lonely. Having Steven there to make sure she was ready for every show, Hank tending to the business details, and being able to count on Vicki for everything else, it was a gift that allowed her to focus on the music. She was fortunate enough to be able to negotiate, or have Hank negotiate, her team into her appearance fees and accommodations.

Even if she had to pay for them out of her own pocket, she would have done it because they made her job and her life easier by being at her side. But there were times like this when the little fame she did have took her away from what she would really rather be doing. She'd have to think of a way to make this up to Bianca.

❖

As they walked the short distance from the Mark to their hotel, Ava kept Bianca's hand clasped in hers. Bianca didn't seem to mind at all.

"Thank you for this evening," Bianca said.

"You're welcome. I'm sorry our dancing was interrupted."

"There is nothing to apologize for," Bianca said smiling. "Like I said, I love watching you play. Sometimes I forget you're famous."

"That may be one of the nicest things anyone has ever said to me."

"It's true. You're an amazing musician and I know people recognize you. But when it's just you and me, no matter what we're doing, you're simply an incredible woman who I'm really enjoying getting to know. I had a nice time tonight."

"Thank you for saying that. I had a great time as well, for the record. I'm sure you'll see more of the city tomorrow with your sister. Where are the two of you having breakfast?"

"Crepes on Cole."

"Oh, yum."

"You know it?"

"Sure. It's a great place."

"Would you like to come with us? I'm sure Elena wouldn't mind."

"That's really sweet. But I want to let you two have time just for you two. I can still leave a ticket for her for the show tomorrow if she's interested. Just let me know either way." *As much as I want to spend time with you, I'm not sure I'm quite ready to meet the family.*

"Okay."

Ava started to get nervous as they crossed the hotel lobby. Obviously, she would walk Bianca to her door. It was right across from hers, so that was a foregone conclusion, but then what? They had a delicious dinner and a fantastic evening. She didn't want to ruin it now by making the wrong move. Once on the lift she stared at the floor indicator. As long as she remembered to breathe she'd probably be fine.

"Are you okay?"

Ava cleared her throat. "Sure. Why?" *Totally not okay.*

"You just got really quiet all the sudden."

The doors opened, and they exited the lift, turning toward their rooms.

"It may sound silly, but I don't want to mess this up."

"What do you mean?" Bianca asked.

"You, me, us. I don't want to ruin it."

"Why do you think you'd ruin it?"

"I don't know. I just don't want to do the wrong thing here," Ava said.

They stood in front of Bianca's door. Bianca pulled her keycard out of her purse.

"So…what would you say if I asked you to come in?"

"Are you asking me?" Ava couldn't decide what she wanted the answer to be.

"Yes."

Ava thought for a moment. Then she reached up and pushed a stray strand of hair behind Bianca's ear. "I would respectfully decline." She cleared her throat suddenly tight with lust. "I do. Respectfully decline. Please don't misunderstand. There is nothing I'd like more than to go in there with you and see what happens. But I don't want to rush anything between us. We have time to do this right."

"Fair enough. Can I get a good night kiss at least?"

"That would be my pleasure." Ava lowered her head. As soon as her mouth touched Bianca's lips it was as though she'd been shot with a low level electric bolt. Her intended gentle kiss quickly turned into a raging inferno. She lost herself. She wanted to recant her previous declination. She stepped back and broke contact. She had to be strong. She had to do this right. "Good night, Bianca."

Bianca blinked several times seemingly trying to focus. She turned and opened her door. "Sweet dreams, Ava. If you change your mind you know where I am."

Ava desperately tried to catch her breath. She watched as Bianca shut the door. Her feet felt glued to the floor. *Am I an idiot? Or am I doing the right thing here? The one doesn't necessarily negate the other.* She spun around and let herself into her room. She needed a cold shower and probably whiskey. Lots of whiskey.

Bianca closed her door and leaned her forehead against it. She let out a long sigh. *Whoa!* She couldn't decide how she felt about being by herself right now. She had not anticipated Ava turning down her invitation. It was very sweet that Ava wanted to give her time. When she thought about it, she was relieved. Their chemistry was off the charts. A little more time to adjust to that might be a stellar idea. *Damn, Ava can kiss.* Bianca was so turned on right now she had some difficulty walking across the room to undress. She removed her dress and hung it in the closet. She unhooked her bra and accidently on purpose grazed her nipples as she was sliding it off. She gasped as her nipples hardened. She wasn't going to get any sleep tonight if she didn't do something about the fire burning between her legs.

She removed the remainder of her clothes and climbed into bed. She thought of Ava and played with her nipples. First softly and then she began pinching and tugging on them. She writhed under her own ministrations and knew it wouldn't be long until she had to take care of the pressure building at her core. She reached down with both hands and spread her lips wide, using one finger on each side to tease. She couldn't hold back the groan that escaped her lips.

Normally, she would have started gently, stroking her clit with featherlight touches, but she was too far gone already. She needed to do it fast. She needed it now. She plunged one finger inside and rubbed her clit with the other. *Harder. Harder. That's it. Right there.* The climax was so quick and so intense her hips bucked off the bed. She gentled her fingers but didn't stop. The second orgasm rolled through her in a gentle wave. She melted into the pillows.

As good as it was imagining being with Ava, Bianca knew her fantasies wouldn't come anywhere close to the real thing. She'd just have to be patient and wait until Ava was ready. Or convince Ava that she herself was ready, if that was what was stopping her. She allowed herself a few minutes to recover. Then she went into the bathroom to remove her makeup and get ready for bed. When she climbed under the covers again, she smiled. *Damn, that woman is in my head. Time for round two.*

CHAPTER SEVEN

Bianca woke early and decided to take a trolley car to breakfast, or at least as close as she could get. Her spirits were high and she was excited to see her little sister. She made it onto the trolley with no difficulty and enjoyed the wind blowing through her hair. She took in the sights around her, but her thoughts kept returning to dinner and dancing with Ava.

She was thrilled when she successfully navigated getting off the moving trolley. She looked quickly at the map she'd pulled up on her phone and headed toward the restaurant. Her heart lifted when she saw her sister out front. She was on her knees loving all over a golden retriever. Bianca strode quickly to them. "Is she yours?"

Elena looked up, a smile lighting her face. "Hey, you. No, but you know me. I can't pass up any canine without saying hello. Her owner just went to grab a coffee inside."

Bianca pulled Elena up for a hug. "I do know that. How are you, sister?"

"I'm great. You?"

"Fantastic."

Elena looked her up and down. "Are you finally getting some loving?"

Bianca laughed. She missed this, the back and forth, the ease of their conversations. She talked to Elena all the time, but it was different in person. Even with video chatting, you missed part of the experience. "Not quite yet, but I'm working on it." *Hopefully, it will happen soon.*

"Hot damn." Elena tugged on Bianca's sleeve. "Let's get some breakfast and you can tell me all about her."

Once they'd placed their orders and grabbed a table, Elena leaned in. "So…tell me everything."

"Well, everything would take all day. Let's just say…Ava and I have agreed to explore the connection we both feel and we're working on what that means. So far we've only had some amazing kisses. She says she wants to take it slow."

"Why did your brows just do that worried furrowed thing? Is going slow bad?"

"It's not bad. It's just…not what I expected. Everything I've read about her led me to think she's something of a player. So why would she put the brakes on when I'm signaling *go* in big neon letters?"

"Maybe you're special."

Bianca guffawed. "I doubt that."

"No, seriously. You said you met her two years ago, but only spent a couple minutes together and she didn't forget you. Maybe you mean more to her than you know. Or…"

"What's the or? I want to know what's behind door number two, please."

"Or maybe you just need to take control. Show her that you really, really want to move to the next step."

"What do you suggest?"

"I'll leave that to you. Use your imagination," Elena said and winked.

"I'll have to give that some thought." Bianca thought about little else when she was around Ava, so it wouldn't be a stretch.

"Is it hard for you at all?"

"Which part?" Bianca asked, pretty sure she knew where Elena was going.

"Wanting to sleep with the woman you're supposed to be writing about professionally?"

"I won't say it's easy." *Well, the wanting part is easy. It's just the rest that gets complicated.*

"Why did you take this job?" Elena asked.

"Needing a job isn't enough of a reason?"

"But you don't. Not really. I saw the will, remember, and the insurance settlement. Karen left you in a really good place financially. If you're careful with your money, you don't ever have to work again if you don't want to. So I can only guess it has something to do with this particular woman? What's so special about her?"

"That's exactly what I want to find out. The truth is I'm exhausted. I'm tired of being numb, of not feeling a whole lot of anything. I have spent more than two years working my way through my grief of losing Karen and our unborn child and there were some pretty extreme emotions in that mix."

"I know," Elena said.

"But ever since I've reached the last stage of loss and moved to acceptance, there hasn't been a whole lot of feeling at all. I walk through my house and it feels so empty and cold. There is no life there. I feel stuck."

"I'm sorry. I didn't know." Elena reached for Bianca's hand to offer comfort.

"It's not something that's easy to explain. Anyway, when I met Ava two years ago, even in the height of my grief, she was able to reach me."

"What do you mean?" Elena asked.

"I didn't really understand it. But when she sat down next to me, I barely noticed. Then, a simple touch from her and the fog began to lift. I still felt overwhelmed and sad, but there was something about the way she was just there. Her presence was comforting and kind." Bianca shook her head. "I know it all sounds a little crazy and back then it scared the crap out of me, but I think she may be exactly what I need to work my way out of this funk. So, to answer your question, I took the job for two reasons. First, I think she is an exceptional woman and musician whose story needs to be told to the world. But I also took it for very personal reasons."

Elena stared at her in stunned silence. Bianca didn't see any reason to hide the truth from her sister. At the same time, she didn't want today to be all about her. Time to turn the tables. "Now, tell me what's going on with you. How's school? Seeing anyone? Talk to any of the family lately?

"Umm, okay. I'm not really sure what to say to most of that. Clearly, you want to shift the focus away from you and your love life. I'll let it drop for now, but I expect updates. So, let's see, to answer your questions, in order…Good. Not at the moment. And pretty much every day, just like you."

"So no lucky woman has managed to rein you in yet."

"Nobody's really tried. But I haven't put myself out there very much either lately. I did go dancing last night, after class, with some friends. Danced with a beautiful woman, but it didn't go anywhere." She shrugged. "Things are pretty busy between school and my clerkship, so it's probably for the best."

"Makes sense. But don't forget to have some fun every once in a while. Life is too short to spend all your time with your nose buried in a book."

She saw the flash of recognition and the slight nod of acknowledgement. She knew they both thought about Karen in that moment and how quickly life could change.

"I hear you. I'll remember," Elena said.

"Good."

"I still think you need to take control and move to the next step with Ava."

"I think you might be right," Bianca said.

They ate and chatted for a while. Finally, Elena pushed her plate away. "So, what else would you like to do today?"

"Other than spending time with you, I didn't have anything specific in mind. I am supposed to ask you if you want to go to see Ava's concert tonight. She said she'd leave a ticket for you."

"And you're just now getting around to telling me this? If it means a chance to meet the woman who has you so twisted up, count me in."

"Twisted up?"

"What would you call it?"

"I don't know, maybe I'm a little off kilter." *On second thought, twisted up might be more accurate.*

"Call it whatever you want. I still want to meet her. Tell her I'd love to attend the concert."

Bianca pulled out her phone to send Ava a text. She got an almost instantaneous response.

"That was quick. What'd she say?" Elena asked.

"She said, 'You got it. Hope you're having a great time with your sister.'"

"That's sweet."

"She is."

"I can't wait to meet her. Now, let's figure out what we're doing with the rest of our day and you can help me figure out what to wear to attend the symphony. I've never been."

"Well, in that case, let's go to your place and case your closet to see if you have something suitable or if we need to move shopping up on the priority list today."

"I like the way you think."

Ava set her phone down on the coffee table in her suite. *Bollocks.* She didn't regret offering to leave a ticket for Elena, not exactly. Part of her was excited to meet someone who knew Bianca so well, but she was family. She had never met any family members of anyone she'd ever dated. She'd never been with anyone long enough to know if they had family, let alone warrant meeting them. Even if she and Bianca hadn't discussed exclusivity, they had been on dates. So that counted. Right? It wasn't like she was meeting the parents, but still. This was Bianca's sister she was going to meet. It felt like a very big deal. She could admit to herself that she was nervous.

Ava traveled around the world for most of the year, every year. While on tour, she was rarely anywhere for more than a week or two at a time, which made relationships nearly impossible; so she didn't really have them. It was easier to keep things light. Until she met Bianca that is. She knew she wanted to get to know Bianca on a deeper level than anyone she'd ever met. But back when they first met, Bianca was in mourning and the timing was all wrong then. That feeling, the understanding that she did want something more with someone had changed things for Ava. The one-night stands and long weekends she had previously enjoyed no longer felt like enough. More often than not these days, she opted for spending her evenings alone.

As she returned to thoughts of meeting Elena, Ava was glad she was sitting down. It was possible she would start hyperventilating at any moment. She was completely overreacting, she was sure. Why was she panicking? She could play in front of thousands of people without breaking a sweat. What was it about meeting Bianca's sister that had her so on edge and nervous? She needed to get a grip. She could do this. She would just be herself and everything would be fine. She hoped.

She was antsy just thinking about meeting Elena tonight. Maybe a run would help. She grabbed her well-worn sneakers from the bottom of her closet and pulled them on. The hills of San Francisco were a little more ambitious than she was up for, so she grabbed her keycard and headed to the hotel gym. An hour on the treadmill should help clear her head.

Thirty minutes later, Ava had reached the three-mile mark, and she was convinced she was blowing things way out of proportion. After the concert they might have time for a late dinner. So, worst-case, she had to make it through two hours or so of conversation. She could do that. She had lots of practice. She was still going strong and as the treadmill gauge reported mile five she began to feel like tonight might even be fun. She shook her head. This was no time to get ahead of herself. She tried to think about anything besides Bianca and Elena for the rest of her run.

Ava blew out a breath. She sat in her dressing room getting ready for the show, and her nerves were back. All because she knew Bianca was in the audience with her sister. Making a good impression on those closest to Bianca mattered to her, and she didn't want to blow it. She didn't even know the proper protocol for this sort of thing. She'd never been in this position before.

Ava didn't really know how to do relationships and expectations. In the past she would see a woman once or twice and then move on. All she knew was that she wanted to be with Bianca constantly, but that made her feel clingy and needy, two feelings she wasn't used to. She hadn't needed another person, maybe ever, if you don't count her parents. Things with Bianca were going well, but she felt like she was going to screw things up somehow.

Concentrate on the music. Just play the music. She could feel her panic receding as she focused on the songs she'd be playing. Getting through the concert was the easy part. She would pay attention only to what she needed to do from the time she stepped on the stage until she took her final bow. She could think about the rest once she made it back to her dressing room.

She looked through the window of the door and found Bianca in the audience. Her nerves finally settled and the tension melted away. She had nothing to worry about. If she could hold on to that feeling, she'd be fine. She glanced at the woman to Bianca's left. The family resemblance was strong. Their facial features were remarkably similar. That's where the physical comparisons seemed to end.

Elena's hair was stylish but short with soft waves. Her shoulders were broader than Bianca's slender physique. Ava couldn't tell from this distance if her eyes had the same intensity as Bianca's, but Elena looked dapper in her suit. Ava's gaze returned to Bianca. She felt the zing of lust she experienced any time she saw or thought about her. *I have it bad for one of the Vega sisters.* She took another deep breath and pushed through the door when she heard her cue. She walked across the stage and stopped in the center. She stood perfectly still for a single breath, looked directly at Bianca, and then raised her violin and began to play.

"Holy crap," Elena whispered. "You didn't mention she was smoking hot."

"Shh. Just watch and listen."

Elena was right; Ava was hot. But she was also sensitive, kind, and caring, all traits Bianca admired. She had listened to Ava's music so many times since they'd first met. Hearing it now with Elena was like hearing it again for the first time. It was still magical and inspiring. Once Ava left the stage at intermission, Bianca turned to Elena. "Isn't she incredible?"

"Oh my God, I've never seen anything like it. I could feel her passion. How you can sit through that for six months…" Elena paused and then looked back at Bianca. "That made me hot. I didn't even know I liked this type of music, but if I had someone like Ava playing, I'd listen to it all the time."

"You're beginning to understand how I feel."

Bianca glanced down when her phone vibrated, then looked at her sister. "How would you like to meet her? She just invited us to dinner after the show."

"Say yes, of course. I need to meet this woman you'll be spending so much time with."

Bianca sent a quick reply and put her phone away as the musicians began returning to their seats.

❖

Ava sat in her dressing room. Vicki was across the room on the settee working on her laptop. When Bianca's response came in, Ava set down her phone. "Vicki?"

"Hmm?" She looked up.

"I need a car after the show and dinner reservations for three somewhere nice."

"Any place in particular?"

"No, it's short notice. See what you can find."

"I'm on it."

"Thank you."

Vicki's gaze returned to her laptop, and Ava was sure she was already working on fulfilling her latest request. Bianca and Elena probably didn't expect anything extravagant for dinner, but they were all dressed up for a night on the town. Bianca was special, and she wanted to show her some of the finer things in life, and this was a singular opportunity to make a good impression with Elena.

She was still extremely nervous about meeting Elena, but she was looking forward to spending time with Bianca and seeing her with family. You could learn a lot about a person watching family dynamics at play. She needed to find out the types of things Bianca liked to do so they weren't only doing what she wanted. One more thing to discover, she mused. She hadn't realized how much fun that could be, but when she'd asked Bianca to promise to answer as many questions about herself as she did, she never imagined how much she'd be learning. There were so many things she wanted to experience anew with Bianca.

CHAPTER EIGHT

After Ava's second set, she returned to her dressing room. Vicki hadn't moved from the settee.

"Everything set?" Ava really didn't have any doubts. She'd seen what Vicki could do in a lot less time.

"Reservations at Chez Panisse in Berkeley. It's supposed to be amazing and it's billed as a Bay Area institution. The car will be waiting for you out front when you're ready. I just sent you a text of the driver's cell number so you can contact her if you have trouble finding her outside."

"Thank you. You're a miracle worker."

"Yes, I am. Will you need anything else for tonight?"

"If you would take my violin and dress back to the hotel, I'd appreciate it."

"Of course, I'll step outside so you can change. Once you're ready, I'll get everything back to your room so you can enjoy your evening with the Vega sisters."

"Thank you."

Ava was thrilled she'd thought ahead and asked Vicki to bring one of her silk pantsuits for after the show. She changed quickly and wiped off the stage makeup. She reapplied a little mascara and lip gloss. She took a deep breath just as there was a knock at the door.

"Come in."

She turned as Bianca entered with a wide smile lighting her face. Elena followed right behind her. Up close, their similarities were even more obvious. "Great show, Ava. The music was beautiful as always, and you are gorgeous. I really like how you look in this suit too," Bianca said as she ran her fingers down the lapels of the jacket.

"Thank you," Ava said. The simple touch from Bianca was turning her on, and she had to take a step back. Now wasn't the time for that, no matter how much she was enjoying it.

"I'd like you to meet my sister Elena."

Ava stepped forward and extended her hand. "Elena, it's a pleasure to meet you."

"The pleasure is all mine, believe me."

"Does that mean you enjoyed the show?" Ava asked.

"I did indeed and the music too," Elena said playfully.

Confused, Ava looked to Bianca who was smiling. "What my sister is trying to say is that she thought you playing the violin was super hot."

"Um, good to know."

Elena threw her head back and laughed. "Ava, you're blushing. I'm sure two women telling you you're hot and sexy isn't new to you."

"Actually, I can't say it's something I'm used to." Ava cleared her dry throat and reached for the hot lemon water. A quick sip helped. "I'm glad you enjoyed the show."

"Oh, you have no idea how much," Elena said.

Bianca put her arm around Ava and looked fondly at Elena. "Since I wholeheartedly agree about your hotness factor, really all the time, I'm going to give her a pass just this once on flirting with you."

It could have been an awkward situation, but the Vega sisters made it an easy and comfortable exchange. Still, Ava was glad Bianca was by her side.

"So, moving on," Elena said. "Bianca tells me you're taking us to dinner."

"Yes, a car is waiting for us out front. How does Chez Panisse sound?"

"Seriously? It sounds great, but how did you get reservations?"

"Vicki has her ways."

Elena looked at Bianca who shrugged. "Don't ask me. I can't figure out how she does anything, but she makes everything so easy."

Once they were outside, Ava led the way to the waiting car. "A limo, seriously? Ava, you sure know how to show a woman a good time," Elena said.

Ava shrugged. "Vicki arranged it. I simply go where she tells me to."

"Is that right?" Elena raised an eyebrow.

They slid into the plush interior, and Bianca scooted close until her thigh was against Ava's. She was thrilled Bianca was so close. "I told Vicki I wanted to treat you both to a special night. Clearly, she carried that through to the transportation."

"It's a nice treat. Thank you," Elena said.

"My pleasure," Ava said.

"I'm curious, Ava, do you play the same music at every show?" Elena asked.

"Oh, no. Each symphony has their own program. There is occasionally a song here or there that overlaps a number of different performances, but from one week to the next it could be completely different arrangements."

"How do you manage that? I mean, from what Bianca's shared with me of your schedule, it doesn't sound like you have a ton of time for rehearsal between venues."

"It certainly gets easier with time. In most cases, I'm familiar with the music being selected and have often played it before. I'm given a list of not only what the entire symphony will be playing, but also specifically what I'm being asked to play. Sometimes that even includes the request to add a song or two of my own, which I enjoy quite a lot. I rehearse on my own between shows, focusing on the ones I either don't know or the ones I need to brush up on. Then I take advantage of rehearsals with the whole group to really polish things before showtime."

"That sounds like a lot," Elena said.

"It's not so bad. It helps a great deal that I love what I do."

"I'm sure it does." Elena glanced out the window as the car pulled up to the curb. "It seems we've arrived. The restaurant isn't much to look at from the outside, but everything I hear about the food is incredible. All of it is locally sourced and organic."

"Sounds wonderful," Bianca said. Elena was right; the exterior certainly wasn't all that impressive. If you were looking for sleek and modern, you would definitely be disappointed. As they stepped inside, Bianca looked around. Then she whispered, "I never would have guessed it was this nice based on the outside."

"Perhaps we're in for a night of delightful surprises," Ava said.

"Indeed," Bianca said.

After they ordered drinks, Elena cleared her throat. "Ava, while we have a moment, I would like to thank you."

"For what?"

"Bianca shared with me all you did for her after Karen passed away. How you helped her. I'm grateful to you for being there for my sister when she needed it most."

"I'm glad if I was able to offer some measure of comfort." Ava turned to Bianca. "But Bianca gave me as much or more that day than I gave her." Ava felt her cheeks heat with the admission. She was glad the waiter appeared to take their order. Once he left, she shifted the focus. "So, Elena, tell me about you. What kind of law are you interested in?"

"I haven't decided yet. I'm leaning toward contracts or tax law. I have this idea that I can help small businesses get set up and running. It depends a lot on where I decide to practice and what I can do in that particular state."

"Maybe I can call you if I ever move ahead with my plan to open a production studio."

"You should definitely do that."

"I'll keep that in mind," Ava said.

"What are you thinking?" Elena asked.

As they ate, Ava shared her ideas with them. She found it fun how they tag-teamed her with questions, each from their own perspectives. It really got her thinking about things in more detail. By the time they finished eating, she felt the plan was much more fleshed out. Maybe her dream was closer to a reality than she'd realized.

Bianca wiped the corner of her mouth with the linen napkin. "Dinner was delicious and dessert was simply decadent. Thank you."

"It really was. I've always wanted to try this place, and coming here with the two of you was very nice."

"It was my pleasure. Thank you for coming. I know you don't get to spend a lot of time together, so sharing tonight with me was generous of you both. It's been wonderful getting to meet you, Elena."

"I feel the same," Elena said.

Once Ava signed the bill, they made their way to the door. Ava had texted the driver as they'd finished and the limo idled at the curb. The driver held the door as they slid in. Ava spoke to her. "We need to drop Elena at her place before we return to the Fairmont. She'll give you the address."

"Yes, ma'am."

Bianca sank into the luxurious seat and sighed. Dinner had been incredible, but she was happiest that the conversation had been comfortable and easy. Elena seemed to genuinely like Ava. She'd ask her more about that when they were alone, but she would have been acting differently if it weren't true. Too soon, they arrived at Elena's apartment building.

They all climbed out of the car. Elena pulled Ava into a hug. "Thank you again for dinner. I'm counting on you to take care of my sister as you travel all over the world together."

When Ava pulled back from the embrace, she made eye contact with Elena. "That's a promise." Then Ava ducked back into the car to give them privacy.

Bianca grabbed Elena in a fierce hug. "I'm so glad I got to see you. I love you. Try to stay out of trouble."

"I love you too. Now go take charge and tell her what to do. You heard her earlier. She goes where she's told." Elena held Bianca at arm's length. They stared at one another, and the moment passed from heartfelt to playful quickly.

Bianca slapped her on the shoulder. "You are very bad."

"But I'm not wrong." Elena chuckled.

"Maybe we'll see about that." The idea piqued Bianca's interest.

Elena laughed. "Safe travels, sister. Keep in touch."

"You know I will."

Bianca watched as Elena let herself into her building before she climbed back into the car. She scooted close enough to Ava that their legs were touching. Ava put her hand on Bianca's thigh. "How was that for you?"

"The whole evening was amazing. But the bigger question for me is how was that for you?" Bianca asked.

"I had a lovely time. I enjoyed meeting Elena. It was nice to see you interact with someone you're so comfortable with."

"I'm comfortable with you too," Bianca said easily, shifting to look at Ava.

"I appreciate you saying that, but I worry that you will meet so many new people as we're traveling that you'll get overwhelmed."

"I'm not worried about that at all. I love meeting new people."

"Really? Sometimes it terrifies me."

"You perform in front of thousands of people every time you take the stage and you're afraid to meet people?"

"I told you the day we met I'm not always very comfortable around people. I have a confession. I was extremely nervous to meet Elena tonight."

"What? I couldn't tell at all. You meet people all the time and all over the world. Why would you be nervous to meet my sister?"

"That's just it, because she's your sister, one of the most important people in your life. It felt like a very big deal and I didn't want to mess it up."

"You did just fine. She likes you. But you don't have to be nervous about meeting anyone close to me. Be yourself and you'll be fine."

"If you say so." Ava didn't seem convinced.

"I do." The car pulled up to the front door of their hotel. "Now, please escort me upstairs so I can get out of these shoes."

"As you wish." Ava stood next to the car and bowed before extending her hand to help Bianca from the car.

❖

As the lift opened on their floor, Ava let Bianca exit ahead of her. "Would you like to join me for a nightcap?"

"I would. That's sounds lovely."

Ava let them into the living room area of the suite. Bianca slipped out of her heels the moment they were through the door.

"What would you like…a glass of wine, a beer, or a cocktail?"

"I'll have whatever you're having. Do you mind if I freshen up a bit?"

"Not at all. Go ahead and make yourself comfortable while I make the drinks."

Bianca went through the bedroom to the bathroom. Part of Ava wanted to follow her into the bedroom and surprise her when she came out. She wanted to be with Bianca in every way, but she didn't want to rush her into a physical relationship. She didn't know if Bianca had been with anyone since Karen died, and she didn't want to pressure her. She turned her attention to the cocktails. When Bianca hadn't returned by the time she'd made the martinis, she started to get concerned. She was about to call out to see if Bianca needed anything when Bianca beat her to the punch.

"Ava, could you come here please?"

"Sure." She set the drinks on the coffee table and hurried into the bedroom. When her eyes adjusted to the dim lighting of the bedroom, she made out the figure stretched out on the bed. Bianca wore a matching set of peach bra and panties and nothing else.

Bianca waited until she was sure Ava could see her. "You can join me over here." Bianca patted the bed beside her. Ava took a couple hesitant steps in her direction. "Wait," Bianca said.

Ava stopped immediately.

"You said you wanted to go slowly. So, I want you to remove your clothes, very slowly."

Ava's eyes widened and she swallowed hard. "That's not exactly what I meant." Ava's gaze moved down Bianca's body. "Are you sure this is what you want?"

"Completely sure. Now, every time you take something off you can take one step toward me."

As Ava completed the slow and tortuous strip tease, Bianca moved closer to the edge of the bed. By the time Ava worked slowly on the buttons of her shirt Bianca sat on the edge of the bed and could reach out and touch her. "Stop," Bianca whispered.

Ava froze, her fingers on the second to last button. Bianca took first one hand and then the other and kissed it. "I'll take things from here." She unbuttoned the last two buttons and slipped Ava's shirt off her shoulders and let it pool on the floor behind her. She lifted Ava's hands and placed them on her own shoulders. Then she looked up into Ava's beautiful face laced with desire and need. Bianca wrapped her hands around Ava's hips and swept up and down her stomach with her thumbs. "You're shaking."

"I'm going to need to lie down soon."

"Soon." Bianca slid her hands up and cupped Ava's bra-clad breasts. She swept her thumbs over the silky material and Ava's nipples peaked and strained against the material. Bianca kissed each peak.

"Bianca..."

"Hmm?"

"I really need to sit down if you're going to keep that up."

Bianca turned them, switching their positions and she backed Ava up to the bed. She removed her bra. "Sit."

Ava sat on the edge of the bed and grasped Bianca's hips so she wouldn't fall back. She looked up and Bianca took that moment to kiss her from above. She gently traced her lips. Then she adjusted the angle and kissed her more thoroughly. Bianca kissed and licked her way down Ava's body. She knelt in front of her and licked and sucked one breast and then the other. Ava writhed under the wonderful torturous attention. She pushed her hands into Bianca's silky hair, trying to hold on. Eventually, Bianca raised her head. "Lie back."

Ava complied without hesitation. Bianca reached for the waistband of Ava's panties and pulled. Ava lifted her hips so Bianca could pull them off. Bianca threw them aside and lifted Ava's legs over her shoulders. Then she ran her fingers through Ava's hot, wet folds. She spread her wide and bent over her. She licked her lips in anticipation, and then she pulled Ava into her mouth.

Ava raised herself onto her elbows so she could watch Bianca. The visual made her even hotter and wetter than she already was. The amazing things Bianca was doing to her with her lips and tongue had her so close to the edge. "Inside, please, go inside," she panted. Bianca slid two fingers into her slick hole while continuing to work magic on her swollen clit. "Oh yes. Fuck." As the wave hit, Ava climaxed so hard she lost all senses for a brief moment. As she came back to herself, her heart was thundering in her chest, her breathing was ragged, everything seemed brighter, and her ears were full of music she was certain wasn't playing on any stereo.

"Wow."

Bianca climbed onto the bed and lay half on Ava as she gently kissed her. "Yeah? Are you okay?"

"I'm so much better than okay. What did you do to me?" Ava asked.

"Only the very tip of what I'd like to do."

Ava raised her arms, limp from the impact of her climax, and pushed Bianca's lustrous hair back so she could study her. "You can do whatever you'd like to do, seriously. But first, I'd like to do a few things to you. She rose enough to capture Bianca's lips with hers.

She rolled them so she was above Bianca, her leg between Bianca's. She could feel her fullness. She deepened the kiss and shifted so she could caress her breasts. She moved her lips down Bianca's body to discover what she liked.

"I'm so ready for you," Bianca said.

Ava lifted her head and studied Bianca for a moment. She had wanted to move slowly, cherish Bianca's body, show her how special she was, but she didn't want to keep her waiting. She moved her hand between Bianca's legs and felt the evidence for herself. "Yes, you are."

She slid two fingers into Bianca, using her thumb to trace her clit, allowing Bianca time to adjust to her fingers. Ava never would have thought it was possible after the climax she had had moments before, but sinking into Bianca made her hard all over again.

"Hmm, feels so good," Bianca said.

Bianca's words brought Ava's focus back to her. She began thrusting her hand slowly in and out. She adjusted to the rhythm of Bianca's hips and increased the speed of her hand to keep up with her needs. Ava was mesmerized by Bianca's face as she approached the crest.

Soon Bianca cried out, "Oh yes, yes, yes."

As Bianca crested, Ava climaxed again. She was so overcome she buried her face between Bianca's neck and shoulder trying to hide all the emotions coursing through her from Bianca. Once she felt she had herself under control, she lifted her head and kissed Bianca. "Was that okay for you?"

"It was amazing."

"Good. I didn't know…"

"You didn't know what?" Bianca asked.

"We hadn't talked about it, and I didn't know if you had been with anyone since Karen, so I wanted to take it slowly to give you as much time as you needed. But I couldn't stop myself from wanting you."

Bianca pushed Ava's hair back from her face like she was trying to see her more clearly.

"I wondered if that was the reason you were hesitating in moving forward."

"You did?"

"Yes," Bianca said. "And to answer your question, you are the first person since Karen. But I knew before we started this trip, I was ready for whatever happened between us. I don't want you to ever question that you made me do something I wasn't ready for."

"You're sure?" Ava could hear the worry in her own voice.

"Oh, sweet Ava, I'm very sure. I appreciate that you wanted to give me time, but the waiting was too much."

"Oh." It was a lot for Ava to take in. She felt extraordinarily special that Bianca had chosen her to be her first after Karen, but what did that mean for them? She couldn't ask that question at the moment, so she decided to focus on the here and now.

"That's why I decided to take things into my own hands, so to speak," Bianca said.

"I'm so glad you did."

"Me too."

CHAPTER NINE

The late morning sun filled the room. Ava cracked her eyes open and let them adjust to the brilliant light as she surveyed her surroundings. Bianca sat at the table by the window, her laptop open in front of her and a breakfast tray abandoned nearby. Dressed comfortably in a tank top and cotton shorts, she was the sexiest woman Ava had ever seen.

As she tapped away on the keys of her computer, Ava studied her profile. She could get used to this, waking up after a night of passionate lovemaking to see Bianca, who inspired such desire and need, at work like this. It might be one of her favorite new ways to start the day. She could only think of one thing that would top it.

She quietly slid out of bed and moved behind Bianca. She wrapped her in her arms from behind and kissed her cheek. "Good morning. Can I convince you to come back to bed?"

Bianca tilted her head so she could see Ava. "It won't take much convincing, but have some breakfast first."

Ava pulled on a robe and dropped into the chair across from her. "When did you get your clothes and laptop?"

"I went across the hall for a few things after I ordered room service. I'm glad they didn't wake you. One of the advantages of a suite I suppose," Bianca said.

Ava picked up the glass of orange juice and took a sip. "Why are you up so early? Did you not sleep well?"

"I wanted to jot down some notes from our conversations over the last few days and do more research for the biography. Since you were sleeping so hard, I thought I'd take advantage of the time.

As for sleep, I slept better than I have in a very long time, but I'm naturally an early riser."

Ava smiled sheepishly. "I usually am too, but I think you wore me out."

"Apparently, we need to work on your stamina."

"Ready when you are to get started on that."

"Eat. We need to keep your strength up. Then we'll play."

"I can't argue with that logic." Ava dug into the lukewarm scrambled eggs. She swallowed and cleared her throat. "So besides, the aforementioned playtime, is there anything else you'd like to do today?"

"Perhaps we could walk around the city for a while and see some of the sights. Maybe have a late lunch."

"We can do anything your heart desires."

"I like the sound of that."

Bianca had just finished dressing when there was a knock at the door. She looked over to Ava who was still drying off. "I'll get it."

Bianca opened the door to Vicki, who did not look surprised to see her. "I'm sorry to interrupt, but I need Ava for a few minutes."

If Vicki wasn't going to act like her being in Ava's suite fresh out of the shower was any big deal, then Bianca wouldn't either. "Sure. Come on in. She's just finishing getting dressed."

"Thanks. How was your visit with your sister yesterday?"

"It was wonderful. I don't get to see Elena enough."

Ava joined them. "Hi, Vicki, what's up?"

"Um, I can go to my room," Bianca offered.

Ava appeared to consider the offer for a few moments, but then shrugged ever so slightly as if reaching a decision. She gestured for Vicki to come over. "No, it's fine. Stay," Ava said as Vicki approached her.

"I need your signature on these checks." Vicki held up the folder she'd pulled from her bag. "I'm sorry to bother you, but you asked that they go out by this afternoon."

"No problem." Ava reached for the folder and Vicki handed it over.

Bianca looked at Ava, then Vicki, and back at Ava trying to discern what was going on. Ava didn't seem entirely at ease with the situation, but after a moment she looked up from where she was signing the checks. "One of the things Vicki does for me is, in many of the cities we play, she finds a few children's and women's organizations that need some financial assistance and I make donations to women's and youth empowerment programs."

"That's very generous."

"It's what I can do."

Vicki raised her eyebrows at that statement.

Bianca nodded. "I'm sure that means a lot to them."

"Well, anyway, even if I'm only in a city for a week or so at a time, this is a way for me to feel more connected and have an impact." Ava finished signing and handed the folder back to Vicki. "Bianca and I are going to do some sightseeing. Do you need me for anything else before we go?"

"I don't. Let me know if there's anything else I can do."

"I think we've got everything covered today. You should take the rest of the day off and enjoy the city."

"Maybe I'll do that. You two enjoy." Vicki let herself out.

Bianca walked to Ava and put her arms around her neck. "Does it make you uncomfortable that I know about the checks?"

"Not really. It's just not something I share publicly. It feels like something private, intimate even. I don't know if that makes sense."

"Can I ask you something?"

"Of course," Ava said.

"I know you said it's a way for you to connect to the cities you're in, but it feels like there is more to it than that."

For once in her life Ava wanted to tell someone the whole truth. She felt guilty for so many reasons. In some ways finding people she could help financially felt like a bit of a penance. It wasn't nearly enough to assuage the guilt she felt about Lara, but after what Bianca had shared with her only days before, she knew she couldn't tell her everything. "I guess it's my way to give back. A part of me feels guilty for having…so much, especially when there are so many who don't have enough just to survive." She opted for a partial truth and hoped it would be enough.

"I think I get it. Thank you for sharing it with me."

"You're welcome. Are you ready to go?" The quicker they moved on from this topic the better.

"I'd like to do my hair since Vicki caught us before I could blow it dry. It should only take a few minutes."

"Take all the time you like. There's nowhere we need to be at a certain time today. Our day is all about doing whatever we want as it comes to us."

"Well, that sounds pretty perfect."

"Good." Ava leaned in for a kiss.

Once they were in the elevator Bianca asked, "Do you have a plan for today or are we literally just wandering around?"

"I thought we could head for the Castro and then check out Haight-Ashbury. Once we're ready for that late lunch, we could eat at Delfinas in the Mission District. I'm open to any and all modifications to this plan and we can definitely stop anywhere you want."

"I'm good with it, but I'd like to reserve the right for changes along the way," Bianca said.

"Brilliant."

"So why the Fairmont Hotel?" Bianca asked as they left the building.

"Well, first, it's one of the nicest hotels in the city. I also like the history of it. Two women had it built to honor their father. Even better than that is when the interior was seriously damaged in the 1906 earthquake, a female architect and engineer named Julia Morgan was hired to repair the building because of what, at the time, was her innovative use of reinforced concrete. There is a ton of history in this area, but that story stuck out to me. So, whenever we're in San Francisco I prefer to stay at the Fairmont."

"Do you have a hotel preference in every city on the tour?"

"Most of them. There is still a place every now and then where I'm trying to find someplace that really appeals to me."

"Is cost ever a factor in your decision? You don't have to answer that if you don't want to. I'm sorry if that was out of line."

"Why? You're asking me everything else about my life, why is money suddenly off limits?"

"I don't know. I guess I just don't know if it's an important part of the story yet."

"You'd be surprised how important it is to my story. I know it and I'm very grateful."

"Why is that?"

"My parents' money allowed me to have opportunities other children never have. They were able to send me to the best schools, for both education and music. Sure, I needed the drive and talent to succeed at those schools, but affording them was never something I had to worry about. They were able to provide me with nannies and tutors when they couldn't be with me.

Even now, most concert musicians don't make enough to live the lifestyle I live. At this point, I supplement with the trust that came to me from my grandmother when I turned twenty-one. I'll come into even more money when I turn thirty-five. I have more money than I know what to do with, and I'm already doing what I love. So, to answer your original question, no, cost is not usually a factor when deciding where to stay."

"Fair enough." Talent, beauty, compassion, and money…Ava really was the complete package. It was hard to believe someone hadn't already snatched her up and taken her off the market. Bianca no longer had to worry about where her next check was coming from again, Karen had seen to that, but she couldn't imagine having more money than she knew what to do with. Ava's wealth was incomprehensible. It shouldn't matter, but it actually made Bianca a little uncomfortable. She wasn't sure why.

"Do you ever wonder if the women you date are after you for your money?" Bianca asked.

"It's never really come up. I have spent time with a lot of women, maybe not as many as the tabloids report, but certainly more than my fair share. The thing is I've never had a long-term relationship before. My lifestyle doesn't make one of those easy. So,

I've never had to worry about why anyone was with me beyond a night or two, a few weeks at the most."

"Oh." Bianca's mind was whirring too much to come up with anything more coherent than the single word. She was focused on the *before* that Ava had used. Did that mean she thought they could have a long-term relationship? Or was she saying she had no interest in one?

"Should I be worried that you're only interested in me for my money?" Ava said it with a grin, but Bianca could tell there was something under the lighthearted tone.

Bianca shook off her deep thoughts. "No, of course not. I'm after you for your body." Bianca was joking, but when Ava frowned and turned away from her, she worried that Ava had taken it differently than she intended. "Did I say something wrong?"

When Ava didn't respond, she touched her arm. "Hey, I was kidding."

"I know."

"Do you?"

Ava finally looked at her. There was moisture in her eyes. "It's just that…"

"What?"

"You're the first person I've ever wanted it to be more than that with. This is about more than the sex for me."

"It is for me too, Ava. I shouldn't have made that joke. You are special to me. It's not about your money, your body, or any other singular thing. It's all of you. Every part of who you are and the connection we have. I'm sorry if I made what is between us feel like less than what it is."

Ava reached out and stroked Bianca's cheek. "It's okay. Really it is. Can we maybe put this behind us and enjoy this beautiful day?"

"I love that idea."

Ava slid out of bed as gently as she could and made her way to the balcony door. She quietly opened the sliding glass door, leaving it open behind her. The cool night breeze felt delicious on her bare skin. She was glad for the dark and the seclusion of the balcony away from any signs of life or intruding light. It was just her and the few stars she could see overhead.

She grasped the railing, trying to stay grounded. Bianca was in her head. They'd had a wonderful day wandering all over San Francisco. After getting past those few awkward moments, they talked and laughed for hours. Then, they'd returned to the hotel and had more mind-blowing sex. Bianca was still asleep in the bed she'd just left.

Ava had awakened feeling energized and knew she wouldn't sleep again right away, even though it was the middle of the night. The cool night air soothed her overheated body. Her mind, on the other hand, was still racing with thoughts of Bianca and how different being with her was than any of her previous experiences.

Ava had never been a touchy-feely person. The women she'd dated before would be shocked by her current behavior. There was something about Bianca. Ava had a near compulsion to touch her as often as possible. Walking anywhere, she reached for her hand. Simply passing behind on her way to the other room, she brushed her shoulder or back. When they sat chatting or eating, she wanted to be close enough to gently squeeze her arm or leg. Whenever she made contact with her skin, as smooth as warm cream, she was soothed deep inside. If Bianca knew the truth about Lara, would she ever let her touch her again?

The secret Ava was keeping felt like an anchor weighing her down, keeping her from being able to truly let Bianca in. Would she ever be able to let go? She stood and watched the lights blink across the distant skyline.

Bianca stirred from sleep as the gentle breeze rustled her hair. She reached to snuggle closer to Ava, but her hand landed on the cold mattress. She woke more fully. Once her eyes adjusted to the dimness enshrouding the room, she saw Ava's silhouette beyond the open balcony door. She rose and pulled her robe on without tying it.

She walked onto the balcony and wrapped her arms around Ava, allowing the robe to shield her from some of the breeze. "Aren't you cold?"

Ava leaned her naked body back into Bianca and moaned as their bodies connected. "Not at all, I'm quite warm still. I'm sorry if I woke you. That's what I was trying to avoid."

Bianca slid her hands slowly up and down Ava's side. "What do you mean?"

"I woke up wanting to touch you, but I didn't want to disturb you. You looked like you were sleeping so peacefully."

Bianca lightly kissed Ava's back and moved her hands around to massage her breasts. Her own center throbbed and her nipples hardened as Ava's breathing changed. "You should never hesitate to wake me if that ever happens again." She gently pinched Ava's nipples to stiff peaks.

Ava gripped the rail harder as Bianca moved her hands south. "Hmmm. Good to know."

"What are you out here thinking about in the middle of the night?"

"Honestly? You and what you do to me."

Bianca slid two fingers through Ava's wet mound, exposing her clit to the gentle breeze.

"Oh God." Ava pushed back into Bianca's center.

Bianca kissed Ava's shoulder and kept working her center slowly, tenderly. "What do I do to you?"

Ava sucked air through her teeth as Bianca grazed over a particularly sensitive spot. "Christ. This. You do this to me. I'm a quivering pile of mush, putty in your hands. You slay me."

Bianca dipped one finger briefly into Ava and then slid it up to circle her clit lightly. "Hmmm. Do you like it?"

"God yes. Please don't stop."

Bianca adjusted her hand, so her thumb could continue working Ava's clit as she slid two fingers deep inside her. "Baby, I'm not gonna stop until you're all done."

Ava sank down on Bianca's fingers and rode them hard. She closed her eyes, blocking out all sensation aside from the scent, sounds, and touch of Bianca. She lost track of time as she thrust herself down on Bianca's fingers over and over until her body went still and she rode into oblivion.

As Ava came back to herself, Bianca was tenderly sliding her fingers over her clit, inspiring gentle aftershocks. Bianca's words came back to her. She laid her hand on Bianca's. "Baby, I'm done."

Bianca's hand stilled. She kissed Ava's neck. "Okay?"

"Hmmm. So much better than okay." Ava bumped back into Bianca, who groaned at the contact. Ava turned and looked at her. "Seems you're still a little ways from okay."

"I'm all right."

"Why would you say that when I'm right here to take care of you?"

"I got a lot of satisfaction from making you come."

"Satisfaction possibly, but not satiation obviously." Ava spun them and pinned Bianca to the rail. "Please, allow me." She crushed her mouth to Bianca's and kissed her deeply. She moved her hand quickly down her body. She left no time for thought, only sensation. She slid through Bianca's wet lips. She was ready. Ava lifted her head, so she could gaze into Bianca's eyes. She plunged two fingers into her but quickly added a third. She pumped into her over and over until she crested and cried out. Watching her face as she orgasmed was the most stunning sight Ava had ever seen.

She kissed Bianca softly. "Better?"

"Yes. Thank you."

"My pleasure."

"Ready to go back to bed?" Bianca asked.

"I don't think I'm sleepy yet."

"Good, that's exactly what I was hoping." Bianca pulled Ava through the doors and to the bed.

CHAPTER TEN

Bianca, Ava, and her entire entourage sat in the airport lounge waiting for their flight to be called. They were flying to Germany. Bianca was much more aware that she was getting on a plane today. Last time she'd been able to block it out for the longest time because everything was so new, but today she was anxious. She was trying to cover her nervousness by asking Ava more questions. Ava laid her hand on Bianca's arm. "Look at me." Bianca met her gaze. "Hi."

"Hello?"

"You don't need to try to hide your fear from me." Ava squeezed her arm gently.

Bianca sighed. "How could you tell?"

"It's not any one thing. I think I'm getting to know you better. Your brow is furrowed, I can tell your shoulders are tense from all the way over here, and every so often you're reminding yourself to breathe. Plus, it kind of gave it away that you just asked me the same question three times." Ava leaned forward as she spoke.

"I guess trying to distract myself with questions wasn't really my best plan."

"Not so much. I've got you. We'll get through this together."

"Thanks."

"So, why don't you let me rub your shoulders and you can tell me about where you would go with your sisters if you could go anywhere for a long girls' weekend."

Bianca looked over to where Hank sat twenty feet away. "Aren't you worried about Hank seeing us?"

"No. It finally occurred to me, he works for me so there's nothing he can do. As mad as I was and still am at him for going behind my back, he brought you back into my life, so I'm grateful for that."

Bianca turned to give Ava a better angle for the massage, which also allowed her to hide her smile in reaction to Ava's words. "Hmm, that feels good. Okay. Well, let's see, a girl's trip, huh? I think that would depend on the time of year. For a long weekend, it would make the most sense to stay in the States, I think. I love autumn in New England. The foliage is beautiful. But we could go to Big Bear in California if we wanted something fun to do in the winter, or we could also do Napa Valley, well, any time of year."

Ava could feel Bianca relaxing as she spoke about all the places she'd visit with her sisters. "Sounds like you'd like to hang out with them almost anywhere."

"Yeah, pretty much. I love them. Sometimes I hate that we live so far away from one another. But I love New England too much to move back to the West Coast."

Most of the time Ava was grateful her family lived so far away. It was easier not to have to face the mistakes of her past every day. The announcement for their flight came over the loudspeaker. Ava felt Bianca tense under her hands. "Relax. You've got this. Let's go together."

"Okay."

Ava reached for Bianca's hand the moment she stood up. "So, is there anything you're looking forward to seeing in Berlin?"

"Pretty much everything. I've never been so I'm excited about all of it." Bianca picked up her bag.

"I still remember my first trip there. It's a wonderful city and we should have some time to explore it together. The thing that stood out to me was that nobody jaywalks. Every single person down to the youngest child waits for the walk signal at the street crossings. Spending so much of my teenage years in New York, it was a stark contrast."

"Why do you think it's like that?"

"I think it's about the culture of following the rules, but I'm not sure."

"Interesting."

They had managed to get into their seats on the plane and Ava had ordered a couple of gin and tonics. Now she just needed to think of a question or two that would get them through takeoff. "What was it that drew you to writing and how did you decide to make it a career?"

"Well, that story could take a while."

"I'm all ears."

Bianca thought for a minute on where to begin her story. "When I first began studying journalism, I expected to work my way up the ranks at a newspaper or a magazine. Later, Karen suggested another option and encouraged me to work freelance."

"Was that something that appealed to you?" Ava asked.

"There were a lot of benefits. For example, I was home more and I got to pick the pieces I worked on."

"Those are great things."

"Yes, they are. I loved it. I probably worked even harder those first few years, because I had to find the work rather than an editor handing me a piece to research or write. But in the end, I get to set my own hours and if I want to work on other projects, such as writing biographies, I get to do that too."

"Sounds like a great gig."

"It is. Freelancing also allows me the freedom to travel since I can write from almost anywhere. But there is still some extra work involved, especially when shopping around a piece or deciding which magazine to approach for a particular story."

"Makes sense."

"I used to travel with Karen on her business trips, so it meant a lot more time for the two of us. The only reason I wasn't with her the day she died was it was only supposed to be a one-day trip down to DC and back."

"I imagine it's very hard to think about that."

"Not as hard as it used to be. I'm trying to focus on the future rather than the past. And right now my job allows me to pick up and travel with you for as long as the job lasts." Bianca was excited to explore new places. Given the brief but thorough tour Ava had given her of Tanglewood and San Francisco, she suspected she was going to be a wonderful guide on this trip, if they had time to play tourist together. Either way, Bianca planned to spend time getting to know all the cities they traveled to.

❖

Bianca glanced at Ava as they climbed from the shower. They'd arrived in Berlin late the night before and had fallen into bed exhausted as soon as they got to the room.

"What shall we do today?"

"I'd love to show you some of my favorite places in Berlin."

"Let's do it," Bianca said.

"I'll ask Vicki to order a driver for us for the day."

"Do you ever drive?"

"Very rarely. Only when I don't have any other choice," Ava said.

"So, I should have been more leery of you driving on our first date?"

"Obviously, but driving the jeep in the Berkshires is about the best driving scenario there is for me. The speeds don't get too high, and I can have the top down and not worry about the air quality. For the most part, I'd much rather leave the driving to someone else and not have to deal with traffic and parking."

"You're fortunate to have that choice."

"I'm fortunate for so many reasons, not the least of which is that you're here with me right now," Ava said.

"Keep talking like that and we might never leave this room."

"Would that be so bad?" Ava couldn't decide which option she would prefer.

"I'm sure it wouldn't be, but I want to see some place that's special to you."

Ava held out her arm. "In that case, right this way, m'lady. Your chariot awaits."

"How long is the trip?" Bianca asked as they settled into the car headed for the Berlin-Dahlem Botanical Gardens.

"Nearly forty-five minutes. The gardens are on the outskirts of Berlin."

"Great." Bianca pulled out her mini-recorder. "How about we make use of the time with some more questions?"

"Lovely," Ava said dryly but playfully.

"I'm going to choose to take that to mean you're agreeable and not with the sarcasm your tone implied."

"Come on then." Ava figured they might as well get the questions out of the way so they could enjoy the gardens.

"What drives you?" Bianca asked.

"You mean besides the driver Vicki hired?"

"Be serious. What compels you to get out of bed every day?"

"Music."

"That is the pat answer and too easy. There has to be something more."

"Why does there have to be?"

"Because there always is. What is it, what makes you get up day after day and lead this crazy life you have?"

Ava looked like she wanted to be anywhere but where she was in that moment.

"Come on," Bianca said. "Do you know you actively avoid meaningful questions?"

Ava thought for a moment. "I guess, honestly, it's the fear of failure."

"What do you mean?"

"Well, I asked for this life. Let's face it, most thirteen-year-old kids don't decide they want to go to school three thousand miles away from home and everything and everyone they know."

"True."

"Once my parents said yes, every day since has been a way to show them that it was worth it. I had to make them proud and be successful, to prove to them and myself that I could reach the expectations I set for myself."

"I'm pretty sure most people, including your parents would say you've more than exceeded those expectations."

"Maybe."

"You don't think so?" Bianca asked.

"I guess most days I do. But I still want to show them that all the sacrifices they made for me were not in vain."

"Seems you made a lot of sacrifices of your own."

"Not that many, I don't think."

"Really? What about any sense of a *normal* childhood?"

"What's normal really? I was doing what I wanted to be doing, what I loved. It didn't seem like I was giving up a lot to go to school where I wanted to."

"Well, you said 'not many,' which indicates you do feel like you made some. What would you say were your biggest one or two sacrifices?"

"Without a doubt, the biggest one has been all the time I have to spend away from my family. If there was one thing I could go back and change, I would find a way to spend more time with Lara and my parents."

"I've been wanting to ask you about when you began touring. You were seventeen when you first started, is that right?"

"Yes."

"Was there ever any discussion that one of your parents should go with you? You were so young."

"Not that I remember. I mean they had just adopted Lara, so it didn't really make sense for them to travel with an infant. I'm not sure it was ever even discussed as an option. I had already been away at school for a while at that point, so it's not like they were with me all the time anyway."

"Right. About school. I put together a timeline. I noticed a bit of a gap where you left school, and it looks like you returned a year later and went to a different school. What happened there?"

"That was a long time ago. Does it even matter?"

"Understanding the things that shape who you are is important. These are your formative years so, yes, it matters."

"Yeah, I get that. I just don't know why something from two decades ago has to have any bearing on who I am today."

Bianca found it interesting that Ava hadn't said she didn't remember. It was as though she was deflecting. Trying to get Bianca to overlook that period of her life. "Maybe it does, maybe it doesn't. I can't really make that call or know if it matters if I don't know the details."

"I'm sorry, but…I'm not comfortable discussing that time in my life."

"Hey, what's going on? After all we've shared, you don't want to tell me about something that happened when you were a teenager? How bad could it be?"

Ava looked like she was going to be sick. "I can't do this. I don't want to. Please, Bianca, let this go."

Obviously, there was more to this than Bianca had realized. Now she had to make a critical decision. One that could cause her to lose Ava's trust if she handled it the wrong way. On the other hand, if she didn't pursue this, was she letting her personal feelings get in the way of her professionalism? If she only ended up writing the article, it probably wouldn't matter at all.

She didn't care to think too hard about the ethics of this while Ava was looking at her as if this point could change everything between them. Did she have to make a choice in that moment? Ava or writing. Was there something from Ava's past that could have such a large impact on the story? Did it matter?

That answer came easier than the others. As Ava watched her with fear in her eyes, Bianca made the only decision she could. "Okay, Ava, I won't dig any further right now. I hope, in time, you will trust me enough to tell me the story on your own."

Ava's sigh of relief was audible. "Thank you. I do want to tell you the story at some point. I just can't do that yet."

Bianca knew she'd made the decision with her heart, and it was the right one for her as a woman, but she wondered how long the reporter in her would taunt her for giving up on the story. She was able to quiet that part of her brain for now by acknowledging to herself that she hadn't let Ava totally off the hook. She'd simply agreed to give her time. That didn't mean she couldn't look later if she decided it was necessary.

CHAPTER ELEVEN

B ianca loved watching Ava on stage. Her confidence in front of massive crowds. The playful exchanges with the other musicians. The way Ava could make her feel like she was playing only for her in a roomful of thousands of strangers. All these things made her feel special. Then there was the way Ava's strong, toned arms played such beautiful music. The brilliant light in her sapphire eyes when she played a particularly difficult piece to perfection, and the way her long, adept fingers worked magic on the violin. Every time Bianca watched Ava make music, every single time, she got turned on.

As soon as the concert ended, she made her way to Ava's dressing room. Bianca walked directly to Ava and kissed her. "Great show, you were fantastic. How soon can we get out of here?"

"Thanks. Um, I need to make an appearance at the merchandise table. Then I'd like to change out of this dress. Maybe forty-five minutes tops."

"Make it thirty and I'll make it worth your while."

Bianca watched as Ava got her meaning and saw the lust and desire in her eyes.

"I'll make that happen."

"Good."

❖

Once Ava and Bianca arrived back at the hotel, they made their way quickly through the lobby and up to the room. The door had barely closed before Ava pushed Bianca against it. She kissed her hard, deliberately. The lust ripping through her couldn't be contained. Bianca was just as frantic. She gripped Ava's shoulder tightly. Ava reached behind Bianca and unzipped her dress and quickly pushed it down. She pushed up her bra, not bothering with the clasp, and pulled Bianca's nipple into her mouth. She sucked it while she squeezed the other breast. Bianca's hips were thrusting, seeking.

Ava plunged her hand into Bianca's panties and slid her fingers over her hot, wet folds. She only brushed her swollen bundle of nerves, causing a moan to escape from Bianca's lips. She drove two fingers into her. She fixed her gaze on Bianca's face and watched her ride to a frenzied orgasm. Ava came with her, still fully clothed.

"Jesus, babe, what was that?"

"Did I hurt you?" Ava asked.

"Hell no. That was amazing."

"I've been so wound up all day. Plus I always have a little extra energy after a good performance. I couldn't help myself."

"I'm not complaining. At all. As previously stated…amazing. I just have one question," Bianca said.

"What's that?"

"Why do you still have clothes on?"

"No idea." Ava started to unbutton her shirt.

"Stop."

Ava froze with the soft command.

"Turnabout is fair play; you undressed me, now I get to undress you."

"Yes, ma'am." Ava's hands dropped to her sides.

"That's better."

Bianca took Ava's hand and led her into the bedroom. She removed her own bra, panties, and shoes that Ava had never gotten fully off in their hasty but delightful coupling moments before. She stood naked a few feet from Ava and simply let her look. She could see the desire burning in her eyes and her breathing grew heavier. It was a powerful feeling to arouse Ava.

She knelt down and removed Ava's boots. Then she slowly drew down her jeans having her step out of them, leaving her panties on for the moment. "Spread your legs just a bit."

Ava complied.

Bianca gently slid her hands up Ava's smooth legs and gripped her bottom. She squeezed and pulled Ava to her. She placed a soft kiss on her covered mound at the apex of her legs. She felt Ava start to quiver. "Patience, darling, we're going to take this very slowly."

"I think I need to lie down."

"Oh you will, but only when I say."

Ava nodded slightly. "As you wish."

Bianca stood and began to unbutton Ava's shirt. She placed a light kiss on each uncovered patch of skin. Ava was trembling steadily now. Bianca pushed her shirt over her shoulders and let it drop to the floor. She studied Ava in her bra and panties. She licked her lips. She wanted so badly to taste her, but she was committed to going as slowly this time as they had gone fast a short time before.

She clasped Ava's hand and led her to the bed. "Turn around."

Ava turned to face the bed. Bianca unhooked her bra. She reached around and massaged her breasts, pressing her own into Ava's back. She worked her nipples into stiff peaks. Without ever lifting her hands, she moved to Ava's panties. She pulled them down so very slowly. Ava whimpered. Finally, she said, "Lie on your stomach across the bed."

"Bianca," Ava's words were a plea, "I need…"

"I know what you need. Lie down."

Ava protested no further. She lay on the bed, face down. Her arms near her head, her cheek against the soft duvet. Simply waiting to discover what Bianca had in store for her was a tremendous turn on all by itself. Her clit throbbed so hard, she was afraid she wouldn't be able to hold out much longer.

She wanted to, more than she would have thought possible. No woman had ever tried to dominate her. She had no idea how hot it would be. Being able to cede control to someone, not having to make every decision. She'd never considered the way that would free up her mind to simply enjoy all that was happening.

She'd never felt more exposed or vulnerable. On the other hand, no woman before Bianca had ever made her feel so secure and safe. Nobody had ever spent so much time showing her how much she was treasured and craved. She was willing to do anything Bianca wanted her to, as long as she didn't stop touching her.

She felt Bianca climb onto the bed and heard herself whimper. Bianca was driving her mad and she wasn't even touching her at the moment. Bianca swung her leg over Ava and straddled her back. Ava sucked in a breath as Bianca's wet center made contact with her skin. "You're so wet."

"You do that to me. Now, close your eyes and relax. Let me take care of you."

Ava shut her eyes and waited. Bianca shifted and her hair shrouded Ava's face a moment before Bianca kissed the side of her neck, her shoulder and slowly, ever so slowly, started working her way down Ava's body. Whisper soft kisses and featherlight touches on the sides of her breasts made her nipples harden more. Soft massages of her bottom, with Bianca's thumb brushing through her slick lips made her center clench in anticipation.

Ava lost all sense of time, but it seemed Bianca was in no hurry. That was fine with her. She could not remember being so worked up before. She loved the journey Bianca was taking her on. But she needed release. Soon. The languid caresses shot pulses directly to Ava's clit, and she couldn't resist any longer. "Please, Bianca."

"Please, what?"

"Please."

"Tell me what you need."

"I need you. Inside me. Finish it. Please."

"Get on your hands and knees."

Ava did as she was told. She stuck her ass in the air, willing to give Bianca anything she wanted. Bianca rewarded her immediately. She thrust two fingers into Ava's slick hole and reached around with her other hand, sliding her fingers through her wet folds until she landed on her swollen clit. "Jesus!"

So many sensations all at once, Ava was overcome. Her body took over and she ground back onto Bianca's fingers. Bianca stayed with her, thrusting into her from one side and fingering her bundle of nerves from the other. Under such a wondrous attack, Ava had no hope of holding out for very long. As the orgasm tore through her she flooded Bianca's hands and collapsed onto the bed. She couldn't move; she couldn't even think for several moments.

The next thing she was aware of was the weight of Bianca on her legs. She had lain across her, apparently to get a better angle. She licked and sucked up all the juices on Ava's well loved pussy. The sexy sounds Bianca was making drove Ava up even higher than before. She thrust her hips to ride Bianca's tongue, and in no time at all she came again.

Bianca crawled up next to Ava so she could see her face. She gathered her close as the aftershocks settled. She kissed her forehead, her nose, and finally her mouth. Ava opened her eyes.

"Oh my God, how do you do this to me every time?"

"What do I do to you?" Bianca asked.

"You leave me completely spent."

"Is that a bad thing?"

"No, of course not. It's fantastic. I just can't seem to keep up with you," Ava said.

"Oh, I think you keep up just fine. You were the one who started this you know. You pinned me to the door when we were barely in the room."

"Oh yeah, I did do that, didn't I?"

"You certainly did. There is something to be said for frenzied and frantic," Bianca said.

Ava rolled onto her side and scooted as close as she could get to Bianca. She kissed her, thoroughly, completely, leaving them both breathless. "There's also something to be said for slow and thorough."

"No reason we can't have both."

Ava rolled them so she lay on top of Bianca. "I like the way you think." She bent her head down for another kiss.

Later, Bianca lay beside Ava, who had dropped off into slumber. She was fully satiated and content. Ava looked even younger at rest. Her always inquisitive, curious eyes were shut. Her full lips were relaxed into a gentle smile. Her golden hair fanned out around her face and created a partial halo on the pillow.

The depth of emotion Bianca felt welling up in her was unwelcome if not completely unexpected. She didn't want what was between her and Ava to be complicated. They were supposed to keep it simple and carefree. Nothing felt easy right now. She was developing real feelings for Ava. She was in danger of losing her heart to Ava. Maybe she already had.

Ava and Bianca entered the reception room together. They maintained a modest distance from one another as this was a work function for Ava. Being groomed from a very young age to handle any social situation with ease and grace, didn't mean Ava had to like them. She wasn't very comfortable with people. Performing for thousands up on a stage was easier than chatting with a small group at a cocktail party.

Unfortunately, she was frequently called upon to do just that. Most of the big symphonies had either before or after parties for their largest donors. This required the musicians, all of the musicians, to mingle. Having Bianca attend them with her made the conversation feel less forced. Everything seemed to be easier with Bianca at her side.

"How about I get us some wine?" Bianca asked.

"I would appreciate that."

Bianca stood at the bar trying to get the bartender's attention. He was busy on the other side of the bar, so she settled in to wait.

When she felt someone tap her shoulder she turned, half expecting it to be Ava. She was surprised to see a stranger next to her.

"Excuse me, are you BJ Vega?"

Bianca was surprised someone was addressing her by name. She looked up to study the woman. She was tall and lanky with olive toned skin and short spiky black hair with a bit of gray at the temples. Her gray eyes were wide with interest. Her wide mouth set in a friendly smile. She was, in a word, gorgeous. "I am, but how did you know that?"

The stranger held out her hand. "I'm a big fan."

"Of mine?"

"Of your writing. But now that you mention it, I could quickly become a big fan of yours," she said with unmistakable flirtation.

Bianca shook her hand. "Thank you for the first, not interested in the second." Bianca turned back to the bar and the woman stood beside her.

"Too bad. I'm Wren by the way."

"Hello, Wren. When I'm not writing, I'm Bianca. Are you with the orchestra?"

"No, I'm a singer."

Bianca looked harder at the woman next to her. "Wait. Are you Wren Stark?"

"Guilty."

"How do you know about my work and what are you doing in Berlin?"

"I've been reading a lot of biographies lately and I came across yours on Etheridge. It was genuine and compelling. I like your style."

"Thank you."

"I'm actually in Berlin looking for you."

"Seriously?"

"As I said, I'm a big fan and I'm looking for someone to ghostwrite my autobiography. I'm hoping you'll agree to take it on."

The bartender arrived and Bianca bought a little time by placing her order for two glasses of white wine. She turned back to Wren.

"I'm flattered, I think, although still a little confused how you found me. But I'm in the middle of a project right now. I don't know when I'll be ready to take on a new book."

"Fortunately, I have no set timeline on my project. Please at least tell me you'll think about it?"

Bianca didn't see any harm in at least considering the possibility, especially since Ava was clearly still reluctant and hesitant to commit to the larger project. "I will think about it."

"Great." Wren pulled out a business card from her pocket. "This has all the ways to contact me. I hope you'll be in touch."

"One way or another I will let you know."

With Bianca at the bar, Ava cast about for something to do. She should mingle, that was her job, but she hated this part. Her team would bring the next donor over for her to chat in a few minutes, she was sure. In the meantime, she was at loose ends and very uncomfortable. Fortunately, she spotted someone she knew. She made her way over to Hendrik, a musician she had met the previous year. As soon as he noticed her headed his way he threw his arms open. "Ava, how are you?"

"I'm well. How are you and the family?" Ava returned the warm embrace.

"All are well. Where have you been hiding yourself this trip? You run off after rehearsal; we haven't had a chance to catch up."

"You're right. We should do that. I have been spending a lot of time with…a new friend."

"Is that the brunette that has been hanging around?"

"Yes. Her name is Bianca." Saying her name made Ava want to lay eyes on her. She looked over to the bar. Her delight in spotting Bianca was short-lived as she saw her blush as she talked to another woman. They appeared to be having a somewhat intimate conversation given how close they were standing to one another. "Do you know who Bianca is talking with at the bar?"

Hendrik glanced over. "Sure. That's Wren Stark. She's made a name for herself in America. She is also becoming quite popular in Europe these days."

Ava didn't like how the tall, dark-haired woman was leaning toward Bianca. A part of her knew she was being a bit ridiculous, but she couldn't seem to stop herself. She breathed a small sigh of relief when Wren walked away.

Bianca turned and watched Wren walk away. She was torn between amusement and confusion by the entire encounter. She picked up the wine the bartender had left behind her and walked over to Ava, offering her a glass. "Hi."

"Hi. Was that Wren Stark you were talking to?"

"Yes. Do you know her?"

"Only of her. How do you know her?"

"We just met. She says she's a fan of my writing and wants me to help her with a project."

"Are you going to help her?"

"I don't know yet, but since she has no timeline in mind, I told her I would think about it."

"I see."

Bianca couldn't tell what Ava was thinking as she looked around the room.

"Look, I think I've been here long enough. What do you say we take off and go back to my suite?"

"I really like that idea," Bianca said.

"Fantastic." Ava took Bianca's hand and guided them out the door.

❖

"Let's do something different this evening," Bianca said as they walked into the suite.

"What do you have in mind?" Ava was intrigued and Bianca had her undivided attention.

"How about we change into our pajamas, make some popcorn, climb into bed, and watch a movie?"

"That sounds perfect."

Once they had changed, they raided the mini-fridge and snack box. They had a virtual feast of junk food between them on the bed. Bianca held the remote. "So do you have any preferences?"

"I have a confession."

"What's that?" Bianca asked.

"I haven't watched a lot of movies. So, anything you pick, there's a good chance I haven't seen it."

"Seriously? How about *The Hundred-Foot Journey*?"

"I don't think I've seen that one. What's it about?" Ava asked.

"If you'd seen it you'd know. You have to see it."

"Okay."

"What about *Under the Tuscan Sun*?" Bianca asked.

Ava shrugged. "Nope."

"*Goonies*?"

"Never heard of it."

"*Tombstone*?"

"Sounds depressing," Ava said.

"It actually has some funny parts, but some parts are sad. How about *Pretty Woman*?"

"I've heard of that one. Julia Roberts, right?"

"Yes. Clearly we need to work on your movie repertoire."

"So educate me."

Bianca tapped the remote against her lips while thinking. "Where to start? That is the question. Shall we start chronologically, by genre, or importance of the film?"

"What's your favorite movie of all time?"

"I couldn't possibly pick just one. Some of my favorites besides the ones I mentioned are *The Princess Bride, Blindside,* and *The Best Exotic Marigold Hotel* but there are so many good ones."

"So, why don't we start with one of those?"

"Makes sense." Bianca played with the remote until she pulled one of the movies up on the screen. "We'll start with *The Princess Bride* because it has a little bit of everything—comedy, romance, drama, magic, action, and more."

"Sounds good."

As the opening credits appeared on the screen, Ava glanced toward Bianca. They weren't doing anything exceptional, simply cuddling on the bed watching a movie. But every moment she spent with Bianca seemed special. She had never been so comfortable with another person. Bianca was already engrossed in the movie. Ava turned back to the screen. She was excited to see what Bianca saw in this film.

What she'd confessed to Bianca was true. She hadn't watched many movies. It felt weird for her to watch a movie alone and she rarely had anyone around that she wanted to spend that much time with. But it felt completely right to be watching a movie with Bianca. Everything with Bianca felt right.

She reached into the popcorn bowl and grazed Bianca's hand. "This is nice. Thank you."

"Thank you for being open to it."

Bianca woke at first light, her body pressed tightly to Ava's. She was already warm and pliant from sleep, but consciousness sparked the lust that was never far away when Ava was nearby. But right this moment, she wanted something more than instant gratification. She gently roused her. "Ava?" she whispered.

Ava turned in her arms and slowly opened her eyes. "Good morning."

"Good morning. I'd like you to do something for me."

Ava snuggled closer. "Sure, what do you need?" Ava started moving her hands languidly up and down Bianca's back.

"I'd like you to play a song for me."

Ava's eyebrow winged up. "Right now?"

"Yes."

Ava studied her for several moments. "Okay, if that's what you want. Let me put on some clothes."

"No."

"No?"

"As you are." Bianca slid out of bed and held out her hand. "Come with me."

Ava took her hand and climbed out of bed. "Where?"

Bianca led them into the living room area and stood Ava beside the ottoman. "Put one leg up here on the sofa." She patted the cushion indicating the spot.

"Like this?"

"Yes. Now wait right there." Bianca strode purposefully to Ava's violin case and brought it back to her. "Here."

"You want me to stand like this and play for you?"

"Yes, please."

Ava opened the case and lifted her violin and bow out of it. "Any requests?"

"No specific song. Play whatever you want, but no matter what happens, try your hardest to keep playing."

"What's going to happen?" Ava's voice trembled slightly.

"Play for me and you'll find out."

Ava began to play. Bianca stood a few feet from Ava and swayed to the music. She lifted her arms and moved in time with the music. She pulled her hands down and fondled her own breasts. She continued moving her hands over herself as though they were a lover's touch. She might have felt self-conscious if she couldn't tell how much touching herself was arousing Ava.

Music filled the room. Bianca turned her back on Ava and bent over, spreading herself wide open, giving Ava a clear view of her. She slapped her own ass, watching Ava's reaction over her shoulder. Her teasing was having the desired impact. Ava's skin was flushed, her breathing erratic, her nipples hard, and her mound glistening. She was fully aroused, but she didn't stop playing.

Bianca moved to Ava then. Her arms moved so gracefully to produce beautiful music on the violin. Bianca reached under Ava's arms to run her thumbs over her fully erect nipples. She gently grazed the sides of Ava's breasts and saw her struggle to keep the rhythm of the music. She removed her hands. "Keep playing."

Once Ava was able to recapture the rhythm that had momentarily escaped her, Bianca knelt in front of her. She watched as anticipation and desire washed across Ava's face. She gripped Ava's buttocks and massaged her cheeks. Ava played on. Bianca sat back on her heels for a moment and simply watched Ava make stunning music. Her own center throbbed. She met Ava's hungry gaze. "Remember, no matter what happens, try your very hardest to keep playing."

"Yes, ma'am."

Bianca leaned forward, stuck out her tongue, and slowly licked up and down Ava's labia. Ava's legs trembled slightly, but the music remained steady. "Good girl." Bianca circled Ava's clit with her tongue, with only the slightest pressure and then backed off. She moved her tongue around Ava's opening and dragged it back up through her folds. Ava's hips were now moving back and forth trying to make contact with Bianca's tongue where she needed it most. The violin remained steady.

Ava found she had to concentrate so hard on keeping the rhythm strong that she was only marginally aware of what Bianca was doing to her. Somehow it made the delicious torture even more exquisite. Normally, Ava could flawlessly play hundreds of songs without much thought. Right now though, she had to keep tremendous focus so she wouldn't disappoint Bianca.

Bianca moved one hand around to massage Ava's bottom. She took Ava fully into her mouth. With her other hand, she thrust two fingers into Ava's slit. Ava almost lost it when all those sensations hit her at once. She managed, just barely, to regain control after missing only one beat. She looked down fearful that Bianca would stop because she had messed up the music. Bianca didn't stop, so she played on.

She was so close. But she had to keep playing. Her body was shaking. She was going to lose it. She gripped her violin tighter and moved the bow faster into an up-tempo to match the feelings racing up her body and coalescing in her center. As she crested, her legs buckled and she fell back onto the ottoman. She wasn't sure how but she was still playing, effectively on her back. Bianca was still feasting on her center and she took her over again.

Finally, Bianca raised her head. "You can stop playing now."

Ava slowed her bow and brought the song to an end.

Bianca took the violin and bow from her and set them gently in the case. Then she helped Ava up from the ottoman and over to the couch where she cradled her in her arms. She kissed her gently, and then tilted her chin so she could face her squarely. "Thank you for playing for me."

"Um, obviously my pleasure."

"As soon as I woke up I knew I had to have you like that. I hope you don't mind."

"Oh, I definitely didn't mind. I'm happy to play for you any time."

"I'll remember that."

CHAPTER TWELVE

Ava and Bianca were in the heart of Paris playing tourist. After hours of viewing Ava's favorite pieces in the Louvre, they emerged into the early evening light. Ava glanced at Bianca. "How are you doing, would you be up for a bit of a climb?"

"What do you have in mind?"

"I'd love to take you to see the view from L'Arc de Triomphe, but it means lots of stairs."

"If you say the view is worth it, I'm up for the climb," Bianca said.

Ava led them through the underground tunnel that would help them avoid the horrendous traffic around the Arc. Before long, they started to climb the curving black metal stairs.

"What are you most afraid of?" Bianca asked once they were making their way up the stairwell.

"I'm not a fan of public speaking," Ava said.

"Seriously?"

"Yes. I can play the violin in venues filled with thousands of people no problem. Just don't put a microphone in my hand and ask me to talk to them. Even talking to twenty people makes me anxious. Honestly, I'm not all that comfortable in small groups either. That's why I enjoy your company so much at the donor functions. It's easier for me when you're nearby."

"I had no idea."

"It's true. Anyway, how about you, what is your biggest fear?" Ava asked.

"Snakes. Definitely snakes."

"Wow, that was a very quick answer."

"I hate them. They're slimy and squirmy and gross. Even talking about them gives me the willies," Bianca said.

"All right, you don't have to talk about them anymore. Besides, we're here."

Ava pushed open the door to the viewing area. After being in the relative darkness of the stairwell, the evening sun temporarily blinded her. She slid on her sunglasses and saw Bianca doing the same. "Just one more large step to get to viewing platform." She took Bianca's hand. "Right this way. You can use the viewfinders if you really want to zoom in on anything, but I love just looking from here."

"Wow. It's amazing how far you can see," Bianca said.

"It's gorgeous at night too. We can wait until the sun goes down so you can see Paris lit up, if you'd like," Ava said.

"As appealing as that sounds, I think I'd rather just head back to the room."

"Well, in that case, we can go whenever you're ready."

Bianca laughed. "I think I can control myself at least long enough to see the view from all sides of the building. Probably."

"Your wish is my command. Right this way."

Ava let Bianca precede her and enjoyed the view of her retreating form. Exploring some of her favorite places with Bianca next to her, made them seem fresh and new. Even now as they looked out over Paris, Ava felt more whole than she had in years.

There had to be more to life than touring around the world playing the same songs for different people. All of the people she was closest to in her life she had met because of her music. Her best friends were her stylist and her assistant. She trusted them immensely, but on some level they were still staff. She'd been touring for more than half her life. What would it be like to settle in one place for more than a month or two? She didn't even have a place she called home other than her parents' house in London.

When the touring was over for the year, she'd always just kept traveling. She stayed for a few weeks here or there, wherever sounded amusing or interesting when she had to make that decision each year. A part of her wondered if she wasn't traveling, how long it would take before she went stir crazy. Another part of her knew she couldn't maintain this pace or lifestyle forever. There had to be something in the middle.

Before Bianca, she'd never considered that she could be happy with one person. Nobody had held her interest for very long. Perhaps that was her. Maybe she hadn't tried to make a connection with anyone because she knew she'd always be leaving. It was always only a matter of time before she had to move on.

What if she had finally found someone with whom she had a strong enough connection that she would never get bored? Someone she could travel with when that was necessary and someone whom she'd want to return home with when the traveling was done? It certainly felt like all those things were true when she thought about Bianca. But would Bianca ever feel the same? Could she if she ever knew the decision Ava had made?

No matter what happened between them, Ava wanted to remember this day forever. She studied Bianca with the sun setting behind her. "We should take some pictures up here," she said.

"Excellent idea."

They snapped several different shots on each of their phones. After spending a few more moments leaning against one another, appreciating the stunning view, they began the descent. When they reached the bottom, they exited the building and Ava steered them toward their hotel.

"Maybe tomorrow we could go see Notre Dame so I could take a picture in front of it for my mom. She'd get a kick out of that," Bianca said.

"If you only want to snap a picture, we can do that on the way back to the hotel. There's a route that will take us right by it." Ava took Bianca's hand.

"That would be great."

"Okay, I'll get us there. Are you still a practicing Catholic?" Ava asked.

"Not really. I go with the family when I'm visiting them just to keep the peace, but organized religion doesn't do a lot for me."

"I feel the same way. There are times though when I'm outside surrounded by nature where it feels quite spiritual and I feel connected…a part of something bigger."

"I know what you mean. The natural world can be so peaceful when you stop and listen. I stopped going to church as a teenager because a lot of the sermons just felt too political to me. I get enough of that when I'm not at church." They had arrived and stood in front of the massive gothic church. "It really is beautiful how the stained glass windows make a Kaleidoscope of color," Bianca said.

Nothing we've seen today compares to how beautiful you are.

"This picture will make my mom happy, thank you for doing this," Bianca said.

"We wouldn't want to disappoint her."

"Well, that's true, but let's get this done because I really want to get you back to the room."

"Then pose, woman. I'll snap a couple pictures and we can get out of here."

"Deal."

Bianca walked through the door Ava held for her. She turned as Ava was closing it. She spun Ava and pushed her back against the door. She crushed her mouth to Ava's. The heat leapt between them like a live wire. Their mouths still connected, Bianca started working the button and zipper of Ava's jeans. Ava wrenched her head away. "Bianca…"

"Shh, baby, I need to taste you."

Ava's moan was all the answer she needed. Bianca slid her hand down inside Ava's jeans and cupped her center. "How are you so wet already?"

"It happens just being around you."

Bianca ran her finger through Ava's slick, warm juices. Ava's head fell against the door. Bianca knelt and pulled Ava's jeans down around her ankles. She glanced up and saw need in Ava's face. She leaned in and traced the path her finger had traveled with her tongue.

She used both hands to expose Ava and then she began to explore with her mouth.

The whimpers and excited sounds Ava uttered spiked Bianca's own arousal to a fever pitch. She held Ava's folds open with one hand so she could reach all of her. With her other hand she pumped into Ava.

"Oh, fuck. I'm so close. Please don't stop."

Bianca wasn't sure she could have stopped if she'd needed to. Ava gripped the doorknob and plunged her fingers into Bianca's hair. Bianca drove her fingers into Ava's hot, wet slit over and over until she bucked and came all over her face. Ava's grip tightened in her hair and Bianca went over the edge with her.

For several moments the only sound in the room was heavy panting as they both struggled to catch their breath.

"Oh my God. If I'd known that was what you had planned, we wouldn't have hung out at the top of the Arc so long."

Bianca stood and leaned into Ava. "There was no plan. I just couldn't help myself."

"Well, I have to say I like what you did there."

"Good." Bianca touched her lips to Ava's. As she deepened the kiss, she ran her fingers through Ava's dripping folds and glided over her clit. Ava came again instantly. Bianca gentled her kisses and held her through the aftershocks.

Ava cupped Bianca's face and stared into her eyes. She felt more for Bianca than she had ever felt for any other woman. She couldn't tell her. Not with the secret still hanging over her. But there was nothing stopping her from showing Bianca how she felt. "My turn."

She kissed Bianca deeply. Then she grasped her hand, walked into the other room, and moved toward the bed. She undressed her slowly, kissing each patch of skin she uncovered. She quickly dispensed with her own remaining clothes. She pressed her naked body to Bianca's and kissed her gently at first. She deepened the kiss and pulled back panting. She didn't want to rush. "Let's lie down."

"Yes, please." Bianca pulled the comforter back and lay in the center of the massive bed. "Come here."

Ava moved onto the bed and lay on top of Bianca, supporting most of her weight on her arms. She lowered her head for another kiss and allowed her body to drop slowly until their naked bodies were fully connected. Ava shifted so her leg was between Bianca's and put pressure on her center. Bianca moaned. Ava finally broke the kiss so she could nip and lick the spot on Bianca's neck that would drive her crazy. She nipped the spot lightly and then licked it to take away any sting. Bianca writhed under her.

"Touch me, Ava."

"Soon."

Ava took her sweet time moving down Bianca's body, spending extra time on all the places she had already discovered that drove Bianca crazy. She found a couple of new spots on her travels which delighted her. Based on Bianca's reaction, she was thrilled to have them revealed. Ava slowly licked her way around Bianca's left nipple and then moved to the right. Then she licked down her abdomen. She kissed her way down and paused to breathe in Bianca's musky scent. She wiggled down to settle between her legs. She glanced up and met Bianca's lust-filled gaze. She spread her open and bowed her head to take her into her mouth.

"Oh God, yes. Right there. Yes."

Ava released her.

"Don't stop."

"Not stopping." Ava lightly licked each side of Bianca's quivering bundle of nerves. Bianca thrashed under her. Ava took her into her mouth again and slipped two fingers inside.

"Yes. Yes. Oh yes."

As Bianca crested, Ava gentled her tongue and fingers and brought her down softly. Once Bianca's body calmed, Ava crawled up to her and tenderly kissed her forehead, her eyelids, her nose, and finally her lips. Then she wrapped her in her arms and snuggled her closely. No words were needed.

Bianca lay watching Ava sleep and couldn't help reflecting on their time together. She enjoyed the way Ava took her hand while they walked. It was different from her experience with past lovers. Karen had always made her feel loved, but she hadn't generally reached out to touch her for no reason. Karen hadn't been one to cuddle on the couch or in bed very often. Ava couldn't seem to get enough, whether it was a gentle touch or brushing by her. Bianca found she liked it very much.

She could go on and on about their differences, even the surface physical traits were disparate. It's what they had in common that really struck her. Their tender hearts weren't obvious to the casual observer. Their compassion for people less fortunate was eerily similar. Their drive and passion for their chosen professions was irrefutable. Their strength, integrity, and resilience in the face of challenges were comparable. There really was no reason to compare them. Karen was gone. Ava was right here, right now.

Bianca knew it was a risk when she'd agreed to join the tour and explore her connection with Ava. She hadn't expected it to happen quite so quickly. But as she watched Ava sleep, she knew it was impossibly true. She was in love with Ava. It was simple and yet so very complicated. She began this trip with her heart wide open. She would not tell her and risk losing her before their time came to its natural conclusion. They hadn't made any promises to one another.

Ava had said this was about more than sex for her, but what did that mean? She certainly hadn't made any declarations beyond that. Bianca could have said something, but she felt like she was in a precarious place already, being a biographer who had fallen hard for her subject. Ava held all the cards here. Bianca had to stick to their agreement and see how it played out.

She would continue with the plan, working on the article and doing research for the potential biography, touring, and enjoying this, whatever this was. When it was done or when Ava decided to end their compromise, Bianca would walk away with her head held high and her heart full. She would treasure the time and memories they were sharing and creating forever. That's what she'd hold on to.

CHAPTER THIRTEEN

The Philharmonie de Paris was still new enough that Ava was thrilled to be able to tour around it with Bianca. It was an architectural marvel. They were headed to see the stage. Suddenly, Ava stopped in her tracks. She was dumbstruck. She couldn't speak, and she couldn't even remember the question Bianca had just asked her. She stood and stared at the man she had been ardently avoiding for eighteen years. Damon Blake was standing less than ten feet from her and there was no escape. He had seen her too. Bianca, standing beside her, looking between her and Damon, probably wondered about her reaction. She'd deal with that later. Right now she had to figure out how to extricate herself and Bianca from the situation as graciously as possible.

Damon strode purposefully toward her, arms outstretched. "Ava Wellington as I live and breathe!"

Did people really say that? Ava shook off the thought. *Focus.* She allowed herself to be hugged but stopped short of returning the embrace with any enthusiasm. "What are you doing here? I thought you were playing in Berlin this week." She was sure Damon was supposed to be the lead cellist in Berlin right now. She couldn't hide her genuine surprise and hoped it came off as that and not the accusation she felt it was.

Her hopes were dashed when Damon gave a short chuckle. "So, I was right. You have been avoiding me."

Ava only stared at him, incapable of doing anything else in that moment.

Bianca stepped forward and extended her hand to fill the awkward silence. "Hi, I'm Bianca Vega."

"Damon Blake," he managed after tearing his gaze from Ava. "Pleasure to meet you."

"How do you know Ava?"

Damon's gaze returned to Ava. "Oh, we go back a ways. Ava and I went to school together in America. We met when, let me see, I think she was..." He looked to Ava for confirmation before continuing. "What, fourteen, fifteen? I was sixteen. It was my first semester. We clicked from the beginning. But we, uh, lost touch. I think it's been about eighteen years since we saw one another." He continued to gape at Ava with fondness as if he couldn't believe he was finally seeing her after all this time.

"Well, in that case, perhaps you and I should sit down. I'd love to hear what Ava was like at that age."

Before Damon could respond, Ava found her voice. "No." She felt both sets of eyes swing back her way at her emphatic refusal. There was no way—No Way—she could let that happen. "Bianca, we need to go." Without so much as another glance toward Damon, Ava grabbed Bianca's hand and retreated back in the direction they had come. She didn't stop pulling her until the two of them were sheltered in the safety of her dressing room.

The moment the door closed, Bianca pulled her hand free. "What the hell was that?"

Ava felt like she was going to be sick. She collapsed onto the sofa.

"Ava, are you okay?" Bianca asked. Her voice sounded very far away.

Ava was so far from okay she was a little surprised her head didn't pop off. Her world was collapsing around her. She had been running for nearly two decades and today her past had finally caught up with her. For years, she had been meticulous in her planning so she could avoid being in the same venue as Damon.

But being with Bianca had distracted her. She had become complacent just when it mattered most. There had been a few times over the years, when they had been perilously close to playing at the same concert. Due to her previous diligence, she'd always managed to use her influence and connections to make last-minute changes so that never happened.

She'd finally dropped the ball, and now she had come face to face with a man she had hoped to never see again. She needed time to figure out how to deal with it. In the meantime, she needed to figure out what to say to Bianca. She needed to defuse the situation because her reaction was bound to have raised suspicions. This is not how she wanted Bianca to find out she had a baby when she was sixteen.

"Ava, are you okay?" Bianca asked again.

Ava's head turned in the direction of Bianca's voice. She seemed to struggle to focus her gaze on Bianca's face. But when she finally did, her features transformed from shock and despair to resolved and detached. "Sure. I'm fine. Sorry you had to see that. Just a blast from the past that took me by surprise."

Bianca drew her hand away from Ava's thigh, stung by the blatant lie. She had no doubt that Damon was more than "just some blast from the past." There was more to this story. But clearly it was something Ava didn't want to share with her. Bianca stood and walked halfway to the door before she turned. "If you're sure you're all right, I'll let you get ready for the show."

Ava looked into her eyes and appeared for a moment like she wanted to say more, but then she nodded curtly and said only, "I'm fine."

Bianca gathered her bag and left the dressing room. She found Steven a couple of rooms down talking to another stylist and pulled him aside. "Would you keep an eye on her tonight? Something's going on and I think she'll need the support."

"What happened? Are you leaving?"

"She ran into an old classmate, Damon Blake." Bianca paused as Steven's whole posture changed, his jaw tightened, and his body went rigid as if preparing for a fight. She desperately wanted to ask him what he knew, but she couldn't put him in that position. "It seemed to upset her quite a bit, but she won't talk to me about it. She says she's fine. She's not. Clearly, she doesn't need me here."

Bianca walked away but turned back at the sound of Steven's voice.

"Wait." He looked like he wanted to say more, but he stopped himself before he gave Bianca any information that wasn't his to share. "Just…Don't give up on her. Give her some time."

Bianca shook her head. "I'm not leaving. I'm only going to the hotel. I'll be there if she wants to talk to me."

❖

The tension between her and Bianca shook Ava for a moment, but she couldn't worry about that now. She had other more pressing matters to tend. She opened the door when there was a knock. She couldn't handle any more surprises today and she wanted to know who she was letting into her space right now.

"Are you okay?" Steven asked.

"Of course I am. Why wouldn't I be?"

"Well, that's bullshit, but we can play it that way if you want." He shrugged when she said nothing more. "Ready for me?"

"Sure." Ava walked over and sat in the chair where Steven was ready to do her hair and makeup.

Steven brushed Ava's hair back from her face and pulled it into a loose ponytail to keep it out of his way as he applied her makeup. She looked into the mirror and met his eyes. "Who told you?"

"Bianca, before she left."

"She left?" Ava braced her hands on the chair ready to stand up and go after her.

"Relax. She didn't leave, leave. She went back to the hotel. She was hurt. She knows something is wrong, but you're not talking so she gave you some space."

Ava blew out a breath of relief. "I can't get into that right now."

Steven was quiet and watched her in the mirror until she met his gaze. "I thought you cared about her."

"I do."

"But you don't trust her?"

"It's not that. I'm not sure I trust myself."

Steven remained silent.

"It's not something I'm proud of, and I haven't told another living soul any of it, since I spilled my guts to you more than a decade ago."

"Maybe it's time."

"I have to get through the show tonight. After that, I'll think about it."

❖

By the time the curtain closed, the throbbing behind Ava's eyes was excruciating. It was all she could do to get through signing CDs. When she finally got back to the dressing room she changed quickly, made sure Vicki had her violin, and left. She didn't want to talk to anyone, and she definitely didn't want to run into Damon again.

Sharing a stage with him after all this time was almost more than she could stand. If she thought she could get away with it, she would have refused to go on tonight, but there was no way that would have been possible without a lot of explaining that she did not want to do. She needed a drink badly. She headed straight for the hotel lounge, and as soon as she sat, she met the bartender's gaze and said, "Two shots of Jack and a whiskey sour."

The shots were set in front of her first. She threw them both back and blew out a breath. She hoped they would start working quickly. When the mixed drink was placed on the bar, she sipped generously. She couldn't remember the show. She'd been too preoccupied with seeing Damon again. She knew she played adequately and the audience had enjoyed the performance, but beyond that most of the night was a blur. She wished the night had never happened. She had hoped never to see Damon Blake again. Given that they were both concert musicians who played the same venues, she knew there was always a chance this might happen. But she had done everything in her power to avoid it for nearly two decades. It seemed her luck had finally run out.

"Can I buy you a drink?"

Ava would have known that southern drawl anywhere. She didn't even have to turn around to know Damon had found her. "No. How did you find me?"

"It wasn't that hard. I just started with the best hotel in the city and got lucky."

"Well, now that you've found me you can go away or go to hell. I don't care which just get out of here."

"Come on, Ava. At least tell me why you're mad at me. I thought we parted on okay terms."

Ava finally turned and looked at Damon. "I'm not mad at you. As for how we left things... You thought what I wanted you to think."

"What the hell is that supposed to mean? Ava, what's going on?"

"It doesn't matter. Now go away. I can't have this conversation with you tonight."

"What conversation? What are you talking about?"

"Nothing, I'm not talking about anything."

Damon stared at Ava, clearly trying to get some idea of what the hell she was thinking.

Ava stood, slightly unsteady on her feet. "If you won't leave, I will."

Damon also stood and gripped Ava's arm. "Wait. If we can't talk tonight, when can we talk? We haven't been on the same stage or even in the same city for nearly twenty years. What's going on?"

Ava took Damon's hand off her arm. "I don't know. I have to figure some things out first." She walked away without another word. She felt Damon's eyes on her until she turned the corner.

Ava should have expected the empty room, but that didn't stop her pang of disappointment that Bianca wasn't there. She had given Bianca a key card to her room and told her to feel free to use it. She could knock on Bianca's door, but it wasn't fair to go to her in her current condition. Bianca didn't want to be with her tonight. As she thought about their last words to one another, Ava couldn't blame her. She'd shut her out, hard and fast. She had a really good reason, but Bianca had no way of knowing that.

She walked to the tall windows and leaned her forehead to the cool glass. The scene below, Paris at night, usually energized her. Tonight she didn't even see it. Her mind drifted back more than eighteen years, to the day she and Damon first met. Their relationship had been brief, but there was no way she could ever forget it. After all, she had a constant reminder.

CHAPTER FOURTEEN

Bianca slept poorly. She was upset Ava had shut her out, but she was torn because she also understood the need for privacy. She already missed having Ava's arms around her during the night. The combination left her restless. When her eyes popped open just after first light, she gave up the fight and flung the duvet back. She dressed quickly and escaped the confines of her room to wander the streets of Paris before it teemed with tourists.

She walked with no destination in mind. She briefly considered purchasing a croissant or a loaf of the wonderful smelling bread fresh out of the oven. Several shops she passed had loaves in the window, but she wasn't hungry and didn't want it to go to waste. As she meandered along the Seine, she didn't really see it. Ava filled her mind and clouded her thoughts. She already cared for her deeply.

Bianca eventually tired of the thoughts circling around in her head with no answers. There was only one person who could give her the answers she sought. The question was whether Ava was willing to share her story. There was only one way to find out. She turned back toward the hotel and quickened her pace.

She disembarked from the elevator and rounded the corner to her room. She stopped short. Ava stood in front of her door, desperately pounding, and her voice was raised enough for Bianca to hear it down the hall. "Bianca, please answer the door, I know you're in there."

"Actually, I'm not."

Ava whirled in her direction so quickly that Bianca nearly took a step back.

"Bianca?" A whisper of sadness and confusion. "I thought you were avoiding me."

"I was out walking. Why don't we go inside?"

Ava stepped aside so Bianca could insert her key card.

Bianca pushed into the room and crossed the expanse to lay her bag on the far table. She took a deep breath before turning back to Ava. The distance between them felt ten times greater than the space separating them. Ava looked lost with her hands slipped into her pockets.

"What can I do for you?" Bianca's voice sounded hollow to her own ears.

Sadness filled Ava's eyes and she took a step forward. "Accept my apology. I'm sorry for the way I behaved last night."

Bianca took a step closer to Ava. "Apology accepted."

Ava sagged in relief until Bianca's next words left her reeling.

"Will you tell me what's really going on?"

"I want to, but…."

"But?" Bianca asked.

She closed the distance to Bianca and grasped her hands. "Please believe me, Bianca, I wish I could tell you all of it right here and now, but it's not my story alone and I need to talk to some other people first. Would you please give me a little time to sort it all out? I promise I will tell you everything when I can."

Bianca looked into Ava's eyes and saw the honesty there. As much as she wanted to know why Ava had been so affected by Damon Blake, she could give Ava the time she asked for. She breathed a soft sigh. "Okay."

Relief blanketed Ava's face. She hugged Bianca tightly. "Thank you." Ava took a step back but gently held Bianca's hands. "May I take you to breakfast?"

"I'm going to have to ask for a rain check. I didn't sleep well and will probably lie back down for a while."

"Would you like some company?"

Bianca gently shook her head, trying to lessen the blow she knew Ava would feel. "Not this morning."

Ava tried to be stoic, but Bianca could see the questions in her eyes. "Okay, I'll let you get some rest then. Will I see you later?"

"Of course, I'll be at the show if I don't see you before that."

"All right, sleep well."

"Thanks. Have a good day."

As Bianca closed the door behind her, Ava blew out a breath. She was crestfallen. Bianca had accepted her apology and said she would give her time to tell her the story, but she left the room feeling more distant from Bianca than she had when she went in. She could only think of one way to make it better, so she needed to get started.

She let herself into her room. She called Vicki. "I need you to track down a number for me." After giving her the details, she hung up. She wasn't surprised when Vicki called her back ten minutes later with Damon Blake's cell phone number. She didn't want to wait until this afternoon, at the hall, to have this conversation. As soon as she had a number, she called, afraid if she waited another minute she might not ever make that call. He answered on the third ring.

"Hello?"

"Damon, it's Ava. We need to talk."

"Name the place and time."

"Where are you right now?"

"Same place as you. Room 706."

"I'll be right there." Ava didn't wait for a response. She hung up, grabbed her key card, and headed downstairs. In less than two minutes, she stood outside Damon's door. She took a deep breath and knocked.

Damon opened the door almost immediately. "That was fast."

"It's important." Ava's words were clipped.

"Clearly." He stepped back.

As she crossed the threshold, Ava's hands were clammy and she had a hard time catching her breath. Her throat felt constricted. "Water." She cleared her throat and tried again. "Could I have some water, please?"

"Here, why don't you sit down?"

"Thanks." Ava sank onto the settee and took a long sip of water.

Damon pulled out the desk chair and sat across from her, simply waiting. When Ava didn't speak and instead stared at him for several moments, he asked, "Ava, what's going on?"

"I need to tell you something I should have told you a long time ago."

Damon looked confused. "Okay."

Ava wiped her palms on her legs. "I imagine you remember the circumstances of our parting ways."

Damon nodded. "Of course. We were young and foolish and I got you pregnant. You left school to take care of it, and then you transferred the following year and I never saw you again. Until last night that is."

Ava stared into Damon's eyes, but her focus was in the past, then she refocused on him. She cleared her throat and spoke in a rush to get it all out. "So the part you don't know, when I said I took care of it…I didn't have an abortion. I had the baby. My parents adopted her."

"What?" Damon leapt to his feet and closed the distance between them and knelt in front of Ava. "What are you saying?"

"We have a daughter."

Ava watched as a range of emotions crossed Damon's face. The joy and excitement were a surprise. The regret and anger were not.

"How could you not tell me?"

"You made it pretty clear that you didn't want to be saddled with the responsibility. You even offered me money to get rid of the baby, or don't you remember that part?"

Damon seemed to rein in his anger and bowed his head with the weight of that memory. "I remember. And I've regretted my reaction many times over the years."

"What?"

"I shouldn't have left you to deal with it on your own. I should have helped you through it, whatever you ultimately decided. It was my responsibility too and I failed you. I've struggled with that."

Ava sighed and released some of the anger she had held onto for too long. "We were young."

"We were, but not so young I didn't know better. I'm sorry, Ava. Can you forgive me?"

"If you can forgive me."

Damon met Ava's eyes. "I think I understand why you did what you did."

Ava studied Damon and finally let go of her anger and some of her guilt. "I did think about having an abortion like we talked about, but when I confessed to my parents how conflicted I was, they offered another solution. I've wondered over the years if I took the easy way out or if I should have made a different decision."

"What do you think now?"

"I think our daughter is brilliant, beautiful, and bold. And she's had loving parents to raise her as they did me."

"I'd like to meet her."

Ava offered a weak smile. "Could you give me a little time with that? She doesn't know about you. She doesn't even know about me."

Damon lifted himself to sit on the settee beside Ava. "I can't imagine how hard it must have been keeping that from her all these years."

"It seemed like what was best, but now I'm not so sure."

"What's her name?"

"Lara, her name is Lara."

Damon breathed the name as if were precious, "Lara." Then he looked at Ava. "How do you plan to tell her?"

Ava shrugged. "I'll think of something. I have to prepare my parents too."

"I'm sure. Oh, by the way, your friend Bianca has been trying to reach me."

"You need to avoid her."

"Why?"

"Because she can't know anything about Lara, at least not until I've told Lara. She's an experienced reporter. If she smells even a whiff of this story, she'll dig until she gets to the bottom of it. I'm afraid she already suspects. I didn't handle seeing you last night very well."

"So why is she here?"

"I could tell you it's because my manager convinced me that getting my story out into the world would help me spread the music to more people. I do believe that to be true. But why is it Bianca's here rather than someone who wouldn't work so hard to find the whole story? That answer is much more complicated."

"Fair enough. I'll avoid her. Just remember to keep me up to date on Lara. I do want to meet her."

"I will."

Ava had been ready for a fight. Damon's response had surprised her and left her head spinning yet again. He even walked her to the door and gave her a heartfelt hug before she left. She hugged him tightly. "I'll be in touch."

"I'm looking forward to it." He really seemed to mean it.

Now that she had unlocked the door to the past, Ava wanted to get it all out in the open. She considered hopping on a flight and trying to see her parents and Lara today, but she knew there wasn't time to have the conversations she needed and be back before the show tonight. Fortunately, the tour would take her to London in three days. Hopefully by then, she would figure out what she wanted to say.

Ava was mentally exhausted by the end of the concert the following night. Her mind had been racing all day. She had managed to get through the show by concentrating on an image in her mind of Bianca. She pretended she was playing only for her. She wanted to be with Bianca tonight, but she wasn't sure if Bianca wanted to be with her. She still felt strange about the way they had left things yesterday.

As she was removing her stage makeup there was a knock at the door. "Come in."

Her heart lifted when Bianca walked through the door. "That was a wonderful show."

"I'm glad you thought so. I was having a hard time focusing. I only got through that whole show because I imagined I was playing for you, to you."

"Well, how about we go back to the hotel and you give me another show?" Bianca asked.

"I'd love to, but I'm afraid I might be too tired. Would you be terribly disappointed if we had a bath and watched a movie tonight?" Ava asked.

"That sounds pretty fabulous to me right now."

"Brilliant."

Bianca gently shook Ava awake as they arrived at the hotel. "Ava, we're here."

"Did I fall asleep on you?"

"You did. You must really be exhausted. Maybe I should just let you get some sleep."

"No, please, I'd really like you to stay with me tonight. I'm sure that little cat nap gave me a second wind."

"All right, come on then." Bianca led the way to Ava's room. "Would you still like a bath?"

"If you'll join me."

"Okay. I'll go start the water. You get undressed."

"Yes, ma'am."

Bianca shook her head. She knew Ava was more tired than she was letting on. Once she got the water temperature right, she plugged the tub and poured some bubble bath the hotel had generously provided into the steaming water. She quickly undressed and went to find Ava. She was sitting on the bed, naked from the waist up, with one shoe off and one on.

She looked up when Bianca came in. "I'm fading a bit. Would you mind helping me?"

"Perhaps we should forget the bath and climb into bed."

"Maybe a short bath?"

Bianca knelt in front of her and removed her remaining shoe. Then she unbuttoned her trousers. "Stand up and step out of these."

Ava complied with the instructions. She reached down, offering her hand to Bianca and pulled her up. "Thank you."

"Right back at you. Now let's get you in the tub."

Once they were situated with Ava in front, between Bianca's legs, Bianca began massaging her shoulders. "You're hard as a rock."

"Yeah, those arrangements were a lot of work tonight. Thank you for this. Your hands are magic."

"You're welcome. Now, relax and let me work out the kinks." Bianca moved from Ava's shoulders to her neck, then down her back and finally returned to her shoulders. Ava's head began to loll and Bianca knew if they didn't get out soon, she'd have a very hard time getting Ava into bed. "Time to get out."

Ava scooted forward and Bianca climbed out first. She was able to help guide Ava when she stood. She wrapped a towel around her and led her back to the bed. "Sit down."

Ava collapsed onto the bed as if her strength had deserted her.

Bianca took another towel and carefully dried Ava. Then with minimal help from Ava, she was able to get her under the covers. She returned to the bathroom to drain the tub and dry herself. Then she turned out the lights and slid under the sheets with Ava. She pulled Ava to her, so her head lay on Bianca's shoulder. Ava was fast asleep.

Bianca wasn't sure what was going on. She didn't think it really had anything to do with tough arrangements. Ava had never been that tense after playing before, at least in the short time she'd been able to touch her after the concerts. She suspected both her exhaustion and stress had more to do with Damon Blake than Ava was willing to share.

Things had changed after he'd shown up. She was concerned that Ava felt like she needed to keep something from her. She considered for a moment trying to figure out what was going on by herself, but she'd said she would give Ava time. So, that was exactly what she was going to do. Maybe in time Ava would trust her enough to share what was happening with her.

CHAPTER FIFTEEN

❖

A va asked the driver to drop her off at the end of the block. She needed a few minutes to settle her nerves and calm her racing thoughts. The walk would help. She had always loved the avenue her parents' home sat on. Each house had a small private garden in back. The sidewalks and shrubbery planted next to them were meticulously maintained year-round. In the spring and summer flowers bloomed from bushes along the street.

She paused on her route now to appreciate the aromas of the summer blooms. Her anxiety ratcheted down to a manageable level. She could do this. She needed to do this. If she couldn't handle this, how would she possibly handle talking to Lara? It was time. She was committed to her plan. Now, she simply had to execute it.

She stood before her parents' front gate and studied the double fronted house. She had so many wonderful memories behind those doors. She hoped with everything she was that her request today wouldn't taint them all. She had to believe her parents would understand and agree with her that this needed to be done. Lara deserved to know the truth.

❖

Ava sat ramrod straight on the settee in her parents' parlor facing them both. She had just dropped a bombshell on them and awaited their reaction. She had no idea how they would respond to her request to tell Lara the truth about her birth parents. As far as she knew she had only disappointed her parents once, and she didn't want this to be a second time.

Her mum spoke first. "Why now? Why after all this time?" Her voice was as gentle and calm as it always was.

"She deserves to know the truth, and I'm finally ready to answer her questions." *At least I hope I am. Either way, it's time.*

Ava's father raised an eyebrow, which showed a lot of emotion for him. "And it has nothing to do with the book?"

Ava sighed. "Not exactly. It's certainly a factor with the timing. I can't let her be blindsided, whether this book ever happens or she finds out some other way. She deserves to know the truth. I would really like to be the one to tell her. She should be able to ask me anything she wants without rumors and inaccuracies muddying the conversation."

"You know you don't have to do this on your own," her mum said. "We've been waiting for you to be ready."

"I appreciate that," Ava said. "I feel like this is something I need to do. In a lot of ways I got away from the whole thing back then unscathed. I need to be the one to explain. If she ends up hating me, she'll still have you both to rely on as we both always have."

"She won't hate you," her mum said.

"I hope you're right, but I worry she will be angry and hurt for quite some time. It's a lot and I don't want to take that lightly."

Her parents exchanged a meaningful look. Her father gave a quick nod. "Fine."

Her mum chimed in. "You can do it your way, but please make sure she knows she can talk to us as well."

"Of course." Ava breathed a sigh of relief. Ava glanced at her watch. Her mother asked, "You don't have to run off right away, do you?"

Ava relaxed into her chair. "I can stay for a little while."

"Good. It feels like a long time since we've seen you," her mum said.

"It feels the same for me."

"You seem different, Ava," her mum said.

"What do you mean?" Ava looked back and forth between her parents trying to get an idea of what was coming.

"Has something else changed?"

Ava released a slow breath. "I've met someone." She couldn't stop the smile that formed automatically as she thought of Bianca.

"She must be very special."

"She is." *You have no idea how much.*

"Will we meet her?"

"It's all still pretty new." Ava would have liked very much to bring Bianca around to meet her parents. However, with things up in the air with the whole Lara thing, plus the fact that she and Bianca hadn't defined their relationship other than exploring their connection, she knew it was too soon. It was probably too early to even be having those kinds of thoughts, but she couldn't help it.

Ava hadn't been this nervous since her first recital more than two decades before. She was finally back in London and Lara was on her way to see her. Ava planned to tell her the truth. Lara deserved to know. But she was scared to death that she was going to ruin their relationship because she had to tell her that she and her parents had been lying to her for her entire life. She wished she hadn't been so afraid of getting close with Lara before now. Maybe then she would have some idea how Lara would react.

She was certain she was going to wear a pattern in the carpet with her pacing. She wiped her sweaty palms on her trousers. Her mouth was dry. She stopped briefly to pull a water bottle from the mini fridge and had just taken a sip when there was a knock at the door. She set the water down and wiped her hands down the front of her slacks again. Ava felt she had on cement shoes as she walked to the door. She was surprised to see Bianca.

"Hey, what are you doing here?" Ava struggled to sound nonchalant.

"I wanted to see you. Can I come in?"

"Now's not really a good time."

"Ava, what's going on? You seem very agitated."

Ava offered a weak smile. "I am actually, quite. Lara is on the way, and she and I have to talk about something important."

Bianca wanted to ask if it was anything Ava wanted to share, but she'd promised her time and space. "Okay, well, I'll be around if you want to come by later."

"Thank you. It will depend on how things go with Lara. If it gets too late, I'll encourage her to spend the night."

"All right." Bianca backed away and turned to walk down the corridor to her room. She tried not to read anything into the fact that Ava hadn't reached out to greet her. As she reached her door she caught a movement out of the corner of her eye. She glanced over to watch a young woman approach Ava's door. She knew it must be Lara, and she was certain she'd never met her but her features felt familiar.

Ava had only just stepped away from the door when there was another knock. She jerked back but stopped before pulling it open. She tried to take a deep breath and settle herself. It was minimally effective. Finally, she opened the door. "Hi, Lara, it's great to see you. I've missed you, kiddo. I'm glad you could make it." Her words tumbled out. She needed to get a grip.

"Hey, sis, good to see you too. You've never invited me to your hotel before without Mum and Dad."

"I know but I wanted to talk to you about something important and I wanted us to have some time just to ourselves."

Lara looked concerned. "Is everything okay with Mum and Dad?"

"Yes, they're fine. Why don't we sit down and we can talk? Would you like something to drink?" Ava couldn't seem to stop babbling.

"No, I'm good." Lara plopped down on the little loveseat by the window and looked at Ava expectantly. "So, what's up?"

Ava smiled inwardly at the show of teenage bravado before she retrieved her water and took a sip, wetting her dry mouth. She pulled out the desk chair and faced Lara, giving her a clear path to the door in case she wanted to leave. Ava cleared her throat. "I asked you to come here today so we could talk about your birth parents." *Real subtle, Ava, like that's not going to freak her out.*

Lara stiffened. "What do you know about it? Why would you not want Mum and Dad to be a part of this conversation?"

"Good questions. I asked them if I could talk to you first, and they asked me to make sure you knew you could go to them with any questions you had about anything. What do I know about it? That's the bigger question, isn't it? I know everything about it. Lara, I am your birth mum."

"What!?!" The incredulity propelled Lara from her seat, but the enormity of the statement seemed to weigh her down and she sat back down, hard. "What?" she asked again.

Ava had seen the panic and pain on Lara's face. She spoke as calmly as she could. She wanted to be clear. This was about Lara not her. Lara deserved answers. "I'm your birth mum. I'm sure you have a ton of questions and I want to answer them all."

Lara opened her mouth and then closed it. Ava could see the wheels turning. Lara was thinking, but she stared into space and said nothing. After several minutes of silence, Ava finally asked, "You all right?"

"Um, no, I don't know," Lara managed.

"Understandable. Would you like to ask me anything?" Ava asked, hoping she could give Lara whatever she needed to know.

"Who's my birth father?"

"His name is Damon Blake. He's a cellist. He only found out about you a few days ago, but he would very much like to meet you."

"I'm not sure I'm ready for that."

"Okay. Whatever you need."

"Why?"

"Why, what? Why did I have Mum and Dad raise you?"

"No, that one I've pretty much figured out. You were young and probably well on your way to a brilliant music career. Why would you want to be saddled with a child?"

"That's only partly true. I was very young, but I also thought Mum and Dad could give you a more stable life and a home full of love." *And they did, but will you ever be able to see that?*

"I'm not even sure I can call them Mum and Dad anymore."

"I hope you can. I know the two of them still want to be that for you. You and I will have to figure out what our relationship looks like going forward, but I gave up any parental rights I had when I agreed to have them adopt you. You had another question though, why what?"

"Why tell me this now?"

"First, because I feel like you're old enough to understand it now and you deserve to know the truth. But also, in the spirit of complete honesty, I didn't want you to be surprised by any of this if someone found out and wrote about it."

"Who would find out if nobody has in more than seventeen years?"

"There's a woman named Bianca. Right now she's writing an article about me, but she might write a biography and if she does, this will inevitably come out. She doesn't know any of this yet, but I'd like to tell her." Ava wanted to tell Lara how special Bianca was to her, but she could see she was already overwhelmed with everything else already on the table.

"No."

Lara's vehemence shocked Ava out of her reverie.

"No?"

"I don't want anyone else to know about this."

"Lara, please…"

"No way, you've had more than eighteen years to get used to this idea. I've not even had eighteen minutes. You can't tell anyone else until I'm ready. Promise me."

Ava met Lara's eyes and silently prayed Bianca would understand. "I promise."

"Good. Now I'm going to send a text to 'Mum and Dad.' I'm staying here tonight and you're going to tell me everything."

"Okay." Ava took the opportunity to text Bianca that Lara was staying the night and she would see her in the morning.

Lara adjusted in the loveseat. "So…?"

Ava moved to the sofa and got comfortable. She suspected they were in for a long night. "What would you like to know?"

"How did it happen? Were you in love? Was it consensual? How did you tell Mum and Dad?"

"I met Damon when I was fifteen and he was sixteen. I'd been at school in America for nearly a year when he enrolled there. We were two of the youngest students on campus and naturally gravitated toward one another, since we both felt a bit like outsiders. He was from the South and felt like a fish out of water in New York. I'm not sure we ever really talked about dating, but we were together all the time when we weren't in class. We even practiced together. I think we were both a bit lonely, and eventually one thing led to another and we started fooling around. I can't say we weren't in love. I mean I'm sure it felt like love at the time."

Ava took a sip of water as she looked at Lara to see how she was taking all this in.

"We were both so into music and our studies that it actually took a while before we decided we wanted to try sex. We were each other's firsts. I didn't really like it, so I didn't want to do it again. From what I understand that's actually quite normal for the first time. But as luck would have it, the condom we used apparently didn't work, because a few weeks later I figured out I was pregnant." In that moment, Ava decided Lara didn't need to know she'd originally thought about terminating the pregnancy unless she specifically asked. "When I went home for spring break a few weeks later, I told Mum and Dad. We had a really long talk, and at the end Mum proposed the idea of them adopting you."

"And you jumped at the chance," Lara said. Ava didn't detect any censure in her voice, but she felt it all the same.

"Not right away actually. I had a lot of questions of how that would work. I also wondered if it would be too hard to be around you knowing I failed you."

"What do you mean that you failed me?"

"You were my responsibility, and if I was handing you over to my parents, it felt like I was giving up on you."

"Or one might say you were giving me a chance at a more stable life," Lara said.

"I hope every day that I made the right choice."

"Well, I can't decide that for you. But I do have a pretty great life. I just hope that now that I know the secret you've been keeping all these year, maybe it means we can hang out more, so I can get to know you for real."

"I'd love that."

❖

Ava walked Lara down to the lobby the next morning. "You okay to get home?"

"I'm fine," Lara said.

"Okay. Look, I know with everything we talked about you might be overwhelmed, but I hope you'll reach out if you have questions or just to chat. No matter where I am I'll have my phone and I'd love to hear from you."

"I will."

Ava had hoped for more but she knew she had to give her time. Even though they'd talked for hours last night, it was a lot to process. "All right, take care. I love you, Lara."

"Love you, too."

It was a start. As soon as Lara left, Ava took the lift back up. She went directly to Bianca's door. She missed her. When Bianca didn't come to the door right away she wondered if she was out for a walk again. That's what she did that morning in Paris after everything happened with Damon. Ava knocked one more time. This time Bianca answered the door. Clearly, Ava had woken her. "Hi," she said through a yawn.

"Good morning, sorry I woke you."

Bianca moved back a step so Ava could enter the room. "It's okay. I was just out late."

"Really, what were you doing?" Only after Bianca raised her eyebrow and stared at her, did Ava play back her question and tone and realize how accusatory it sounded. "Sorry. That came out wrong. I just wondered how you spent your evening."

"Well, since you were busy, I had to find my own fun."

"Bianca..."

Bianca finally smiled. "Relax, I'm playing with you. I went sightseeing. Did you have a nice time with Lara?"

Ava blew out a breath. "It was...fine."

"Sounds exciting," Bianca said blandly.

"Actually, I'm not really sure what I expected, but she's still talking to me so that's something."

"Why wouldn't she?"

"Uh, yeah, about that, Lara asked me not to say anything to anyone else about what we talked about. She needs some time with it. I'm sorry but I promised."

"Okay. That wasn't cryptic or anything."

"Look, there is a complicated family situation that I really need to keep confidential for now. I hope you can understand that." She really hoped this wouldn't change things between them.

"I can understand that, but I can keep a secret if you need someone to talk to."

Ava wished it was that simple. "I'll keep that in mind, but for now can we talk about something else? I've missed you. Where did you go sightseeing?"

"First, I went up in the Eye. London is beautiful from that vantage point. Then I went to the Tower of London and strolled by Big Ben and Buckingham Palace. You know, a lot of the touristy things. I thought about taking a bus tour, but it seemed like too nice of a night to not be out walking."

"Sounds nice. I wish I could have gone with you."

"That would have been nice, but I'm sure you've seen it all before."

"Sure, but not with you."

"Well...maybe next time."

"I'd like that."

Ava moved to Bianca. "I'd like to kiss you now."

"Well, okay," Bianca said.

The kiss was weird. Something was off, different. Ava found herself holding back. She broke the kiss. "Where would you like to go to breakfast?"

"Where's your favorite place for breakfast? We are on your home turf."

"There are so many good places. But I'm particularly fond of Balans. It's a short walk from here."

"Sounds perfect. Let me just hop in the shower real quick and I'll meet you in your room is say twenty minutes."

"Right." Ava crossed the room. She looked back once she'd opened the door. "See you then."

Ava wasn't sure why she hadn't suggested joining Bianca in the shower. Something just didn't feel right. Maybe she was coming down with a cold or maybe she'd just stayed up too late talking with Lara. Or it could be she'd just been through an emotional wringer. Whatever it was, she hoped she figured it out really soon because Bianca was in there right now getting all wet and soapy and she was missing it. She didn't want that to happen very often, given the choice.

Maybe going to breakfast would help them reconnect. But she had to be careful not to talk about Lara too much. She didn't want to break her promise, and if she started talking about Lara, she might let something slip. She could not let that happen. She would have to think of other things to talk about. That hadn't ever been a problem with Bianca before. Why did it suddenly feel like a very big deal?

CHAPTER SIXTEEN

By the time Bianca let herself into the room, Ava had showered and was feeling much better about everything. There were plenty of other things they could talk about. It would be good to have some alone time with Bianca. She strode purposely into Bianca's space. "I don't think I gave you a proper hello this morning."

"So what are you going to do about that?" Bianca asked.

Ava pulled Bianca to her and crushed her lips to Bianca's. When Bianca opened her mouth, Ava answered the invitation with her tongue. She got lost in the kiss for several moments. Then she remembered herself and stepped back, breaking the kiss. Bianca was panting as hard as her, trying to catch her breath.

"Wow. That was a much better greeting."

"Good. Now how about that breakfast I promised you?"

"You get me all riled up and you still want to leave the room?"

"Well, we need to eat, but I'm certainly open to finishing what I started after breakfast."

"You'd better be. I suppose I don't mind the anticipation."

"Lovely. Shall we?"

As they rode the lift down to the lobby, Ava decided now was as good a time as any to share the news with Bianca. "So, my parents are coming to see the show tomorrow."

"Oh, how nice. Do they come see you play a lot?"

"At least once every time I'm in London. They've also traveled to see me a number of times."

"Wonderful. I'd love to meet them."

"I suspect you'll get that chance."

"Great. I have a ton of questions for them."

"Of course you do."

Bianca paused in her walk across the lobby and studied Ava. "Do you have a problem with me asking them questions?"

"Not a problem per se. I guess I just don't really see the point. Can't I tell you everything you need to know about me?"

Bianca began walking again. "Getting the perspective of the people closest to you will give me a better overall picture of you and your life. It makes for a better story. Your perspective is great for an autobiography, but for a biography I need to talk to more than just you. We've been over this."

"I know. I suppose it's easier for me to forget about the book when you're only asking me questions, you know, I can pretend we're simply getting to know one another or its just for the article. When you start talking about involving other people, it gets more real."

"I'm not sure what to say to that."

"Not your problem. I'll figure it out." Ava was silent for several moments. "I don't mind you talking to my parents. They're looking forward to meeting you as well."

"Do they know about us?"

"Not specifically. I've told them I've met someone. I never said a name or indicated it was you. They know you're working on the article and that you might write the biography. That's all they know for now. Would you like me to tell them?"

"Let's leave it how it is for now. There's no point in them knowing about our personal relationship at this point."

"Okay."

After breakfast Bianca felt like they were back on the same page. She was looking forward to some time alone with Ava. They held hands on the way back to the hotel, something that had been noticeably absent on the way to the restaurant. Ava seemed to have a lighter step too. Maybe she had figured out whatever had been bothering her this morning.

They were alone in the elevator. Ava moved to her and kissed her. If the ride hadn't been quite so quick, Bianca might have tried for more. She was still in a lust induced haze when the elevator opened and they walked out. The lingering sentiment evaporated as Ava quickly pulled her hand away from Bianca's as though she'd been burned.

Bianca looked up and saw Lara sitting against Ava's door. She had her head back and her eyes closed, so Bianca was pretty sure Ava didn't need to worry about her having seen anything. But she wasn't sure why Ava would be worried about that with her sister anyway. They hadn't discussed it, so who knew what her reasons were.

Bianca took advantage of Lara's ears being covered by headphones. But she still kept her voice down when she turned to Ava. "I guess we'll have to take a rain check on the sexy time."

"I'm sorry. I didn't know she was coming back so soon."

"It's not a problem. Clearly, she missed you as much as you miss her."

"Thanks for understanding. I'll catch up with you later?"

"Sure." Bianca glanced down before kissing Ava quickly on the cheek. "Enjoy your time with your sister. Do you mind if I meet her?"

"Of course not."

Ava was more than a little surprised to see Lara. When she'd walked her out earlier this morning she hadn't expected to see her again until tomorrow when she joined their parents for the show. But nothing had really gone as Ava had anticipated since Paris, so maybe it was time she start getting used to her new normal.

She stood over her, but when her shadow didn't jar Lara, she bent down and shook her shoulder. "Lara?"

She blinked a few times, adjusting to the lighted hallway. "Hey." She stood quickly looking between them.

"Lara, this is Bianca. Bianca, this is Lara."

Lara nodded. "Sure, the biographer you told me about. Hiya."

"It's nice to meet you Lara. I hope you two have a nice day."

"Thanks," Ava said. She watched Bianca let herself into her own room. Then she turned to Lara. "Want to come inside?"

"Sure."

"Want anything to drink?"

"A Coke would be good."

Ava grabbed a couple bottles from the mini fridge. "Here you go."

"Thanks."

Ava waited to see if Lara would initiate the conversation. She had shown up, so she had something on her mind. But when she simply sat drinking her soda and looking around the room, Ava decided to intervene. "So, what's up?"

Lara shrugged. "Just felt like hanging out longer. I have a few more questions. Is now a good time?"

Ava sat across from Lara. "You're welcome to hang out with me whenever you like. You are also allowed to ask me any questions you have any time you want."

"Really?"

"Yes. In fact, if it's okay with Mum and Dad, and you're interested you could even come with me on tour until your classes start again."

"Really? You wouldn't mind me tagging along?"

"Truly, I would welcome it. I feel like I have spent too much of your life too far away because it was so hard for me to be near you and not feel guilty."

"You feel guilty?"

"Sometimes, yes. Don't get me wrong, I know I made the best possible decision at the time. I couldn't have asked for better parents for you. But there is still a part of me that felt like I should have stayed around more. Helped with you more. Spent more time with you and gotten to know you better." Ava looked at Lara.

"All right, I get that on some level, but I've also realized you were a year younger than me when you had me. I can't imagine how freaked I'd be if something like that happened to me. So, I get it. I get why you reacted the way you did. Maybe you should start giving yourself a break and start getting to know me now."

"You're a brilliant young woman, Lara." Ava was proud of who Lara had become.

"Well, I got that from somewhere and whether it was from my birth parents or from Mum and Dad, you had a hand in that."

"I don't know what to say to that, but I would really like to get a chance to know you better. So, will you think about coming along on the tour for a few weeks?"

"Sure. I'll think about it."

"Great."

"By the way, I had a good chat this morning with Mum and Dad," Lara said.

"That's really great to hear." Ava was relieved Lara was at least willing to talk with their parents. It would only help in the long run if she felt like she could communicate with all of them.

"Yeah, it was nice. But they couldn't fully answer one question for me."

"What question is that?"

"Who else knows about me?" Lara asked. "They weren't sure who else you may have told."

Ava was relieved she knew the answer to this one. "Aside from Mum and Dad, the lawyer they hired to take care of the adoption paperwork." Ava started mentally checking them off as she thought back. "The midwife who delivered you at the house, although she wouldn't have known anything about the adoption, I don't think, only that I gave birth to you. Your birth father, Damon, as of a few nights ago. And Steven. That's all, as far as I know."

"Steven? Why did you tell him?"

"Because he's a good friend. The night of your seventh birthday, after spending the day with you, when I had to leave I was sad, deeply sad. I called Steven and he took me out for a drink. I got wasted. I just didn't want to feel everything I was feeling for a little while. Anyway, when Steven was trying to get me back to my hotel, I told him the whole story. He's never breathed a word to anyone and he never will."

❖

Bianca knew she would be a nervous wreck if she thought about meeting Ava's parents in any capacity other than as her biographer. As long as she could remember it was a part of the job, she'd be fine. Andrew and Grace arrived a little while ago. Ava had wanted her to stay in the dressing room with her to greet them, but she felt it was better to give them all a few moments as a family. Plus that way she could keep everything on a more professional level. She took a deep breath and braced herself outside the dressing room. It was time to meet the Wellingtons. She knocked.

"Come in," Ava said.

Bianca opened the door but hesitated before entering. The room seemed to burst with people. She took a moment to look around and realized there were only four others in the room besides Ava. Ava's parents both had a big presence. Her dad was physically big. He could have easily have been a rugby player in his youth. She'd have to ask him about that. Her mom was tall and slender, like a dancer. She had a charisma radiating off her that seemed big enough to occupy its own space. Steven was busy putting the finishing touches on Ava's hair. Lara was lounging across the room on the sofa playing on her phone, seeming to ignore everything and everyone else in the room.

Bianca strode into the room. She thrust out her hand. "Mr. and Mrs. Wellington, I'm Bianca Vega, Ava's biographer. Lara, it's nice to see you again. Ava's told me so much about you all. It's so nice to finally meet you in person."

Bianca noticed Lara's eyes dart to Ava who shook her head slightly. Lara's head went back down to her phone. *Weird.*

"Bianca, it's lovely to meet you as well. But please, we're Grace and Andrew," Grace said as she returned Bianca's handshake warmly.

"I have so many questions for you both."

"Why don't you come for tea tomorrow and we can chat."

"That would be wonderful."

"It's settled then, and of course you're coming for supper at our home after the show tonight."

Bianca glanced at Ava who met her gaze and nodded.

"Absolutely, that sounds lovely."

"Terrific."

Grace had apparently invited everyone in Ava's travel family for the after concert supper. They began with cocktails in the honest to goodness front parlor. Andrew made the drinks behind his well-stocked side cart. The room was comfortably sized and elegantly decorated. Bianca imagined in the winter, a fire raging in the large fireplace would be quite a lovely touch.

She glanced around the room. Vicki and Andrew seemed to be having a lively discussion about a local soccer team. Bianca couldn't help but think of it as soccer even though her parents referred to it as football. Grace and Steven were discussing something decorating related that Bianca couldn't quite follow. Ava was chatting quietly with Lara. She wanted to check in with her. They had ridden over with Steven and Vicki so there hadn't been a chance. Now there were too many curious eyes around. It would have to wait until later.

A discreet bell rang. Grace stood and cleared her throat. "Dinner is ready. Shall we move into the dining room?"

Bianca took the opportunity as everyone was moving to get next to Ava. "How are you doing?"

"Lovely. It's fantastic to have everyone in one place. How is this for you?"

"It's wonderful. I'm enjoying watching you with your family."

"In a professional or personal capacity?"

"Both."

The Wellingtons' dining table easily sat the seven of them with plenty of room to spare. Bianca turned to Grace. "You have a lovely home. This chandelier is stunning."

"Thank you. We picked that up in Italy a few years ago. If you'd like, after dinner, I could give you the full tour. Show you the room Ava grew up in and a few other spots you might enjoy hearing about."

"I would love that, thank you."

Ava overheard the conversation between Bianca and her mum. A part of her was thrilled they were getting along so well. The other parts of her were conflicted. She felt like she was hiding so many things these days. She couldn't tell Bianca about Lara. She hadn't told her parents how much Bianca was starting to mean to her.

They didn't even know Bianca was anything more to her than her biographer. And she was hiding her feelings for Bianca from Bianca herself. She had lived with one secret for more than half her life. That had been hard enough. In the course of a week, she now had more than she could keep track of. Something was bound to break.

It wasn't fair to tell Bianca about her feelings when she wasn't yet able to be completely honest with her. Maybe letting Bianca interview other people in her life would give Ava the time she needed. She knew her mum was better equipped than she was to keep the secret discreetly under wraps no matter how many questions Bianca threw at her.

Hopefully, Lara would lift the ban before Bianca came asking questions again. She could only hope. She looked at Lara who was sharing something with Steven. He was laughing hard. Maybe Lara would share the story with her later. She felt like it had been a long time since she'd laughed so freely.

As dinner was served, Ava tried to relax. Everyone was having a great time, but her mind was still spinning with how to move forward with Bianca with the secrets hanging over her head.

Later, as they were getting undressed in Ava's hotel room, Bianca wrapped her arms around Ava from behind. "Are you okay? You got really quiet at dinner."

"I'm fine. I just have a bit of a headache."

"Would you like a massage?"

"Hmm, no thank you. As nice as that sounds, I think I'd like to get into bed, cuddle with you, and close my eyes. Is that all right?"

"Sure, that's fine. I'm pretty wiped out myself."

They slid under the sheets. Ava sighed when Bianca wrapped her arms around her as the big spoon. She was going to have to figure out something soon. She couldn't keep making excuses. Her body wanted so badly to be with Bianca. But her heart wouldn't let her as long as she was keeping secrets from her. It had been different before Damon and Lara knew the story. She could rationalize in her head that it was only fair they know first.

But now, even though it wasn't true, if felt like everyone in her life knew the truth except for Bianca. It wasn't fair. Once she had brought the secret out in the open, she had wanted to share it with the woman in her life. If she did, she'd destroy the bond she was building with Lara. It was a no-win situation. But this wasn't Lara's fault, and she owed it to her to abide by her wishes.

When Bianca accepted the invitation to tea, she assumed Ava would be joining her. But apparently, she and Lara had other plans today. Bianca would have some quality time with Ava's parents all alone. They were lovely people who had opened their home to her last night. As long as she remembered to keep on her professional hat, she should be fine. When she rang the bell, she half expected the door to be answered by a maid or butler. She was pleasantly surprised to be greeted by Grace. "Bianca, so lovely to see you again. Do come in and please make yourself comfortable."

"Thank you for having me back so soon."

"It's our pleasure. Andrew will be down in a few moments."

They moved to the front parlor where they'd had cocktails the night before. This afternoon there was a full tea service set on a cart by the settee. Bianca sat where Grace indicated and set her bag down by her feet. Grace took one of the chairs across from the sofa.

"Now, Bianca, what have you seen since you've been in London?"

"A number of things, I spent an evening sightseeing. Is there anything specific that you'd recommend?"

"If you've never seen a show in Piccadilly Circus, you should get Ava or Steven to take you. It's similar to your Broadway, with London flair, of course."

"I'll keep that in mind." Bianca thought it could be fun to see a show.

Grace looked over Bianca's shoulder. "Ah, here's Andrew now."

Bianca went to stand, but Andrew waved her down. "Please sit. It's nice to see you again."

"Likewise."

Grace began preparing the tea. "How do you take it, Bianca?"

"A little milk, please."

"Right, here you go." Grace handed her a delicate cup. She had arranged biscuits along the edge of the saucer.

Bianca sipped the tea. "Oh that's wonderful." Once both Andrew and Grace had their tea, Bianca cleared her throat. "I guess I'll jump right in with my questions if that's all right."

"Certainly," Grace said.

"What was Ava like as a child?"

"Curious and inquisitive about everything," Grace said.

"Shy and quiet," Andrew added. "She loved being outside more than almost anything. The only times she could tolerate being inside were when she was practicing her violin or reading, and she would take those outdoors as often as possible."

"She was all those things and so much more. We knew very early on that she had a special talent, but we wanted to keep as much of her childhood as normal as we could for as long as that was realistic," Grace said.

"Whose idea was it for her to study in America?"

"Definitely hers. As I said, we were trying to keep her home life normal," Grace said. She looked at Andrew and then back to Bianca. "We knew when she brought it up we had to let her go. That's where she felt she could get the best training, so she was willing to subject herself to the big wide world and so many new people."

"She was so young. Weren't you worried about her?" It was clear to Bianca how much Ava's parents loved her. She wondered how hard it had been for them to let her go so early in life.

"All the time, I stayed in a hotel down the street from her school for most of that first year in case she needed me for anything. But as the year wore on, she needed me less and less."

"What was that first year like for her?"

"Almost her whole life was about music then, and she seemed quite capable of managing that on her own. I would spend longer and longer periods away from her to see how she did. I knew if she was going to eventually perform professionally I wouldn't always be able to be with her. But we still kept a nanny nearby whenever I was away so she wasn't ever completely alone. As mature as she was for her age, she was still only a teenager."

"Sure, that makes sense." Bianca couldn't quite wrap her head around what that must have been like for Ava. Basically on her own from the time she was so young. She thought about what she'd been doing at that age and could not imagine not having her parents and siblings with her every step of the way. But it didn't seem appropriate to get into all of that with Ava's parents. Maybe she'd ask Ava about it later.

"Now may I ask you a question?" Grace said.

"Like mother, like daughter. If I didn't know better, I never would have guessed Ava was adopted."

"What do you mean?"

"She and I have an agreement that she can ask me as many questions as I ask her."

"I'm not surprised. As I said, she has always been very curious." Grace seemed amused.

"Anyway, please ask me anything you want. Either of you."

"In that case, I'll go first," Andrew said. "What are your intentions toward our daughter?"

"Excuse me?"

Grace laid her hand on Andrew's thigh and answered for him. "Please excuse him. We've never actually met anyone Ava's been interested in. He's a bit overprotective. But it was quite obvious to us last night, based on the way you two were looking at each other, that you're more than Ava's biographer."

Bianca felt like a fish out of water for several moments. She couldn't breathe. She could feel her cheeks heating up. She decided the best way forward was total honesty, well, almost the complete truth. "You're right. Ava and I are seeing one another, but it's too early to define our relationship. If I may be perfectly frank, I care about your daughter a great deal. She is an extraordinary woman. I don't know where things will go, but I will treasure whatever time I have with her."

Bianca wasn't quite sure how she'd managed it, but Grace had smoothly moved them back on track after their little detour and they'd patiently answered her questions about Ava for more than an hour. They were a gracious, compassionate, and humorous couple. Even the way they shared the back and forth of storytelling showed the teamwork their marriage was built on. Part of her envied their easy companionship. She had thanked them, welcomed the hugs both of them offered. She left knowing she would likely never see them again. It made her a little sad, but it was just the way it was.

CHAPTER SEVENTEEN

Bianca was out of sorts. She was confused and flustered. Things had changed so much between her and Ava after Paris. There was more tension between them and not the good kind. Ava seemed stressed all the time, which was completely unlike her. She wouldn't talk to Bianca about what was bothering her no matter how many times she offered.

Since the night Bianca met Ava's parents, Lara was around all the time. Even stranger, Steven tagged along too. Lara stayed over in Ava's suite most nights. Bianca hadn't been able to get Ava alone for more than a few minutes in days. Ava invited her to join them and she had a couple of times at first because she thought it would be a good opportunity to watch Ava and Lara interact. But she ended up feeling like the fourth wheel on a tricycle. The three of them seemed to have inside jokes and stories she wasn't privy to. Even without all that, she didn't want to try to have a private conversation when Lara was in the next room. So she kept to herself. She went sightseeing on her own. She didn't have anything new to add to her notes, so she spent some time outlining an idea she had for a novel.

Tonight though, she had agreed to watch a movie with Ava, Lara, and Steven in Ava's suite. Once the movie ended, Lara said good night and conked out on the couch. It was amazing how quickly teenagers could fall asleep.

Steven stood first. "That's my cue to leave. Good night, ladies."

Bianca stood and glanced at the couch. "Hang on, Steven, I'll walk you out. I'm headed that way too."

Ava rushed over. "Wait, Bianca. I was hoping you'd stay for a little while."

Steven looked between them. "I'm going to let the two of you figure this out," he said as he turned for the door.

Once the door closed, Bianca focused on Ava. She didn't say anything at first. That ever-present tension was smack dab in the middle of them. Ava didn't seem to have any words either. Finally, Bianca broke the silence. "So…I'm going to go."

Ava bowed her head slightly, almost in defeat. "I'll walk you out."

"I'm right across the hall. It's not necessary."

"Please?" Ava said.

"Fine."

Bianca turned outside her door. "Well, good night."

Ava leaned in for a hug. It was beyond awkward. "Could we maybe go in and talk for a minute?"

"Why? What's the point?" Bianca asked.

Ava looked shocked.

"You haven't wanted to talk to me in any real way since the day Damon Blake came back into your life. Now you're hiding behind your sister. So what could you possibly want to talk about now?" Bianca had lost her patience and it all came tumbling out.

"I don't know. I just thought…"

"What? You thought you'd come in for a quickie? A little lovin'? That's not working for me, Ava."

"What are you talking about?"

"Don't pretend you don't know."

"I'm sorry we haven't had time for us lately," Ava said.

"You could fix that you know. You could set aside some time for us to talk or just do something, just the two of us. Or maybe what was between us has just come to its predictable conclusion. No hard feelings?"

"I don't think we need to make that decision right now," Ava said.

"Why not now?"

"Because it's late and we're both tired. We shouldn't make any hasty decisions."

"It may seem quick to you, but I've had days to think about it. No point in the delaying the inevitable," Bianca said. Meanwhile her heart was hurting at even the possibility that this was the end.

"What are you talking about?"

"Look, I know I said I could give you time to deal with whatever family stuff you have going on, but that was before I knew it would mean you ignoring me. I can't do this anymore."

They stared at one another for several moments. Finally, Ava shook her head. "I'm sorry. I don't want to fight with you and I don't want you to leave. I know it's been a little crazy having Lara around all the time. But we're getting to know each other, kind of for the first time, and I'd feel bad sending her away."

"Okay. I get it. You're working on your relationship with your sister. But I'm supposed to be working too. I haven't been able to make any real progress in days because you haven't had time to talk to me. Not to mention the fact that you refuse to answer any questions."

"I know. I just need a little more time."

Bianca had heard enough. "Fine. You do what you need to do. I'm going to bed. Good night."

"Good night, Bianca." Ava stood while Bianca shut the door. It felt like she was being shut out. She was losing ground in the relationship she'd been building with Bianca. She was stuck and didn't know how to get out of this murky situation. She felt guilty as hell keeping this secret from Bianca. It was strange that she felt guiltier now than she had in all the years she'd kept the same information from Lara. How did that make sense?

The worst part was she missed Bianca badly. It wasn't even about the sex they were no longer having. She also missed spending time with her, doing things with her, seeing the world through her eyes. She loved their time at the Louvre and the botanical gardens in Berlin. Even more than that though, she missed the emotional and physical connection they had.

She wasn't feeling it anymore. She knew it was because she'd thrown up figurative shields so Bianca couldn't breach the secrets she needed to protect. As long as she had her force fields raised, she wasn't going to be able to reconnect with Bianca. There was no way she could lower her defenses and trust she wouldn't do irreparable harm to the relationship she was building with Lara.

Until Lara lifted the embargo, Ava would simply have to figure out a way to live with the situation. She had to give Lara whatever time she needed to deal with what she'd shared. After all, as Lara had pointed out, she had eighteen years to digest the information. Keeping this secret from Bianca was weighing on her mind and spirit.

She had gotten herself into this mess and nobody was going to help her figure a way out of it. For now, she'd keep doing the best she could to contain the damage and keep everyone relatively happy. She wasn't doing such a great job on that front with Bianca. She let herself back into her room. She checked on Lara to see if she had everything she needed. She was burrowed under the covers on the couch, snoring lightly. She looked so young and innocent with her features relaxed in slumber. It struck Ava that her own mother had probably never seen her like that at that age.

When she was Lara's age, she was already traveling the world as a solo violist and her mother was in London raising Lara as her own daughter. Ava came back to the moment. She was glad Lara didn't have the stress and worries she had at her age. At least someone would get some sleep tonight. She turned out the lights in the living room. Then she went into the bedroom and shut the door lightly.

"Ava, darling, you clearly aren't sleeping," Steven said as he put on her foundation. "I'm going to have to work extra hard to hide these bags under your eyes."

"I'm sure you've got some magic up your sleeve to make me fit for the stage," she said without trying to hide her sleepless nights.

"Oh, hon, you're always beautiful and nothing is going to change that. But talk to me. What's keeping you up? Or should I guess? I couldn't help but notice a bit of tension as I left last night."

"As always, your penchant for understatement is truly amazing."

"Did you two lovebirds manage to work it out?"

"Quite the opposite, actually. She's unhappy that we don't have any time together."

"So make some time."

"It's not that easy."

"It could be. I could entertain Lara for the evening. She's been wanting to see *Alien*."

"Look, I appreciate the thought. I really do. But it's more complicated than that."

"Because you're afraid?"

Ava met his eyes in the mirror. "Lara has only ever asked one thing from me."

"Have you checked in with Lara lately? She seems pretty okay with everything. Maybe she wouldn't mind you telling Bianca now."

"No. It's too soon to even broach the subject."

"So what are you going to do?"

"I have no idea. He spun her chair so she could look in the mirror.

Ava took in her appearance. She turned her head one way and then the other to study Steven's work. "You're a miracle worker."

"I do what I can."

The smirk on his face told Ava her compliment had resonated. At least she was doing something right.

Bianca was at loose ends. She decided to play tourist and explore Piccadilly Circus. Perhaps she'd stop and see a show as Grace had suggested. As soon as she exited the Tube stop, she felt a bit like she was at Times Square in New York. There was so much to see. Most people around her seemed to be happy and carefree. She was trying to be those things, but it was difficult not to think about Ava. Those thoughts weren't making her happy right now. She tried to focus on the excitement around her.

As she was walking down the street, someone called her name. She spun around to see who it was. She was surprised to see Wren jogging over to her.

"It is you. What are you doing in London?" Wren asked.

"What, you're not still keeping tabs on me?"

"Touché. No, I figured you had my info, if you were interested I would hear from you, if not…" Wren shrugged. "My loss."

"Fair enough. To be honest, I haven't really considered your offer yet. I have a lot going on with my current project," Bianca said.

Wren looked at her watch. "Would you like to grab a coffee now? Just to talk about what I have in mind. No pressure, but it might give you a better sense of the project."

"Sure, why not?"

They walked around the corner to a restaurant Wren suggested. They were seated quickly. It made Bianca think briefly about the service Ava received everywhere they went together. She wondered for a moment when she became the person who hung out so casually with celebrities, even sought after by them if her present company was any indication. When did life get so strange? She shifted her focus back to Wren. "So, what's your vision?"

"I want a book that is genuine first and foremost. Something that not only looks at my singing career, but also explores my activism and other aspects of who I am. I want something that reflects my beliefs and values, not just the polished persona the world tends to see. I'm a proud feminist. I want younger generations to realize they can achieve great things no matter where they began their journey."

As Wren spoke, Bianca found herself drawn to her charisma. Not in a sexual or romantic way, but in an "I could see myself becoming good friends with this person" kind of way. "That sounds like an authentic project. Why aren't you writing it yourself?" Bianca's couldn't help but compare Wren's transparency and desire to be honest to her current predicament with Ava.

"I write songs and I love being a songwriter, but the idea of even trying to write a book isn't appealing to me."

"I see."

"I know I need help, so I decided to find a writer I identified with and that's you."

"I'm flattered and I must say I am intrigued by the project."

"Does that mean you're interested?" Wren asked hopefully.

"I'm not ready to commit just yet. I couldn't start anything until I'm done with my current project, and the extent of this project is still unclear."

"There is no set timeline for this project, so if you're willing to write it, we can work around your schedule." Wren was everything Ava was not as far as a cooperative collaborator. The contrast was stark.

This was sounding like an attractive next project. It would give her something to focus on after things ended with Ava.

"Can I ask you a personal question?" Wren asked.

"I suppose."

"What made you sad just now?"

"You're quite observant aren't you."

"It makes me good at what I do. Are you avoiding the question?"

"I was just thinking about my current project ending," Bianca said.

"You must be really attached to it."

"I'm in love with her actually," Bianca said without thinking and was surprised by her own words.

"Oh wow. Does she know?"

"I haven't told her."

"Maybe she feels the same way. I assume we are talking about Ava Wellington?"

"You know her?"

"Not personally, no. I certainly know who she is and I saw the two of you together in Berlin. It may not be my place to say this, but based on the way she looked at you, I'd say it wouldn't hurt her feelings if you told her the truth."

"I can't. Especially right now, things are just too…complicated," Bianca said.

"I'm sorry to hear that. If there's ever anything I can do, even if it's just be a friendly ear, you know how to reach me."

Bianca knew Wren was genuine. It wasn't a move or a strategy. Working with Wren would be energizing. "I appreciate that very much."

"Why don't you come see my show tonight?"

"You're playing tonight?" Bianca asked. "Here?"

"Yes to both."

Bianca couldn't think of any reason not to accept the offer. It wasn't like she had any other plans. "I think I would enjoy that, thank you."

Wren's show was amazing. Unfortunately, it had done little to take Bianca's mind off Ava. Bianca had watched Wren and knew no matter what happened with her and Ava, she and Wren would never be anything more than friends. It made her more comfortable thinking about working on her project. She didn't want to be in a position again where she had to doubt her own professionalism. In that way, the night had been a success.

Now, as she rode back to the hotel with the car and driver Wren had offered, her thoughts returned to Ava and what she was going to do about her. No matter how much or how often she thought over things, she couldn't resolve the contradictions. It was becoming clear the only conclusion for this relationship was heartbreak for Bianca. And the project would end with an article.

Ava and Lara lingered over breakfast in the hotel restaurant. They had sat so long they virtually had the place to themselves. Ava was reading the news and Lara was listening to music. Lara removed her earbuds and looked at Ava. "We should go shopping," Lara said.

Ava put down her tablet and focused on Lara. "We should? Why is that?"

Lara looked around briefly to see who else might be listening. "I don't think I can ever think of you as my mum," Lara said softly.

"Okay?" Ava wasn't sure what to say or where this was going.

"I mean I understand you gave birth to me, it's still weird on some level, but I get it. But you've always been my sister, Ava. For more than seventeen years that's who you've been to me. Is it okay if that's how I still think of you?"

"Totally okay. If that's what works for you, I'm completely on board. I just want to be in your life and spend time with you."

"Which is why we should go shopping."

"I'm not making the connection."

"It's something sisters do together, right?"

"Yes, I believe it is," Ava said. *Sisters.* It seemed Lara had defined their relationship after all. Ava was relieved on more than one level. Lara was obviously getting more comfortable with the situation. Also, even though Ava had always known how she and Lara were really connected, after all this time it was easy and natural for her to think of Lara as her sister. Now that Lara knew everything, there was nothing keeping them from forming a deeper bond. One they would make by choice, not circumstance.

CHAPTER EIGHTEEN

After having gone another whole day without hearing from Ava, Bianca reached out to Steven and invited him to lunch. She waved to him when she saw him enter the restaurant. He strode over and sat.

"Hey."

"Hi. I'm glad we could finally do this," Bianca said.

"What is it we're doing exactly?" Steven seemed suspicious.

"We're having lunch." Bianca held up the menu she'd been studying before he arrived.

He picked up the menu in front of him. "Yes, but there's more to it than that," Steven said.

Bianca waited until the waiter took their drink order to respond. "I'm spending time with the people closest to Ava to gain insight into her life from different perspectives."

"I told you once before you wouldn't get a lot out of me. I won't betray Ava by telling anyone about her life."

"She's fortunate to have such a steadfast ally in her corner."

"Now you're just trying to butter me up."

"I'm not. I really believe that."

The waiter returned to see if they wanted to order food. They made their selections. Then Steven leaned his elbows on the table. "So, I guess there's not a lot to talk about then."

"Well, hang on. What if we talked about you instead?" Bianca asked.

"Me? What do you mean?" Steven looked skeptical.

"For example, if I were to ask you how you came to work for Ava, would that be something you'd be comfortable talking about?"

Steven pondered the question for a few moments. "I suppose."

"Then let's start with that." Bianca could see the wheels turning as Steven thought about the story.

"It's quite embarrassing really."

"Why is that?"

"Well, it involves a reality television show called *Salon Wars*, a hair dryer, and a dumpster."

"I'm all ears."

By the time Steven finished his story, Bianca was laughing so hard her sides hurt. If the rest of the conversation went this smoothly, she might actually make some progress.

"Can I ask you a question now?" Steven asked.

"Sure, it only seems fair."

"Why are you so down lately?"

"What do you mean?" Bianca tried to deflect. She knew exactly what he meant, but she had no desire to betray Ava either.

"I think you know. Ever since Paris, things have been different. Even I can see it."

"I'm not sure we should talk about this."

"Look, I get it, believe me I do," Steven said. "Let me offer a bit of unsolicited advice."

"If you must."

"Give her some time."

"What do you mean?" Bianca felt like she'd given her nothing but time.

"She's not used to having to share focus on more than one person at a time. Having Lara around is new for her, and I'm sure she's struggling with figuring out how to spend time with you too."

"Has she always led such a solitary existence that she really doesn't know how to balance her time with multiple people?"

"Think about all you know about her and her life at this point. I'm pretty sure you already know the answer to that."

"I hadn't really thought about it like that." Even when she did, Bianca wasn't sure what to do with it. Ava knew she was waiting on her to decide on the larger story. If Ava couldn't even find time to work with Bianca on the article, what was she even still doing here?

Bianca's pleasure from her meeting with Steven was short-lived. She'd written up her notes in under an hour. She needed Ava to participate to make progress. She tracked her down the next afternoon, after rehearsal ended. "Ava, can I have a word?"

Ava looked surprised to see her but recovered quickly. "Sure, what's up?"

"I need some time with you. My progress has stalled. I think it would help if I could ask you some more questions."

"Look I can't right now. I have plans with Lara."

"If not now, when?" Bianca suspected if she let Ava leave without answering her she could go another couple days without hearing anything from her.

"I'm not sure."

"I guess I can continue to interview the people closest to you. Steven was a big help. Maybe I could speak with Lara. You know, get an insider's look from the little sister." She knew Ava disliked the idea of her talking to other people, so she hoped this would convince her to pick a time they could talk.

"That's not necessary. How about we meet for lunch tomorrow?"

"Fine. I'll come to your room around noon." Bianca hated this tension between them. She couldn't figure out what had changed, but it didn't stop the fact that she still had a job to do.

"Okay. I really should go now. See you then."

Ava walked away. There was no way she was going to allow Bianca and Lara to be alone together. She wasn't crazy about the fact Bianca had forced her hand. But it was a clear choice. She needed to protect Lara. She owed her that much. But maybe if she could be there with her and Lara was comfortable with the idea, it wouldn't be so bad.

As far as lunch tomorrow, maybe she could have Vicki find a noisy restaurant that made the conversation difficult. She couldn't believe she was going to these lengths to avoid true dialogue with Bianca. Things had certainly changed quickly between them. The onus for that was squarely on her shoulders, but she didn't see a way around it.

Lara wasn't ready for her to say anything. She had no choice but to continue to remain mute about anything to do with Lara or Damon for fear she'd reveal the secret. But surely she could make it through one lunch. She cared about Bianca. Certainly they could find something else to talk about.

❖

When Ava got back to her suite, Lara was lounging on the sofa staring at what appeared to be an action movie on the television. Ava sat on the chair nearby and stared at the screen without really seeing anything. Her mind was still spinning from her encounter with Bianca. She wasn't sure how long she sat there, but eventually she noticed the noise had stopped. The movie was over. She glanced over at Lara who was studying her.

"You all right?" Lara asked.

"Yeah, I'm all right."

"Really? Because you just stared into space for the last forty-five minutes."

"Oh, I didn't realize. I ran into Bianca after rehearsal. She wants to talk with you."

"About what?"

"Me. She wants to interview you. But you don't have to if you don't want to, I can tell her no."

"Do you not want me to?"

"It's not that. I just feel like…I should protect you."

"Do I need protection from Bianca?"

"That's not what I meant. But Bianca has an uncanny ability to get people talking about things, and I don't want her to make you uncomfortable or put you in a position you're not ready for."

"You didn't tell her anything about…you know."

"About me being your birth mother?"

"Yeah."

"No, of course not. You asked me not to and I won't say anything until you're ready."

"About that…" Lara said. "I think I might be ready to start telling people."

"Really?" Ava had mixed feelings about this news. On the one hand, if Lara was comfortable enough to share this information, it meant she had accepted it and was ready to live life with this as the new normal. But it also meant Ava no longer had an excuse to keep it from Bianca. She wasn't sure *she* was ready to tell her. Ava was still quite concerned about how Bianca would react to her having given up her daughter. She hoped Bianca would be compassionate about the fact she was so young and it had been the best option for Lara. But…she couldn't know that for sure.

Lara shrugged. "Yeah, I think maybe I am."

Ava thought for a moment about how best to respond. "You can take some more time if you need it. There's no need to rush into anything."

"Maybe you're right. I feel like telling Bianca might take the story out of our hands," Lara said.

"That's always a possibility. But, she's not likely to ask you about any of that."

"In that case, I'm pretty sure I can handle some questions. But if you want, why don't you tell her I'll only do it while you're in the room?"

"That wouldn't be weird for you?" Ava felt like a coward that she hadn't taken the chance to get Lara onboard with telling Bianca the truth. But she needed a little more time.

"No. She wants to ask me questions about my sister, right?"

"Yes, that's what she said."

"Then I have no problem with my sister being there."

"Okay. I'll let her know." Ava took out her phone and sent Bianca a text. After receiving an immediate reply, she looked up at Lara. "You okay doing this right now?"

"Sure. Why not?"

"All right, she says she'll be over in a few minutes."

Quicker than Ava expected or was ready for, there was a knock at the door. She went to answer it and let Bianca into the suite.

Bianca walked in and made eye contact with Lara. "I appreciate you agreeing to this on such short notice."

"Sure," Lara said. "Why don't you have a seat and we can get started."

"Okay." Bianca took the same chair Ava had just vacated.

Ava found her tablet and sat at the table nearby. She wanted to be present but not in the way. From this spot, she could hear the conversation but not be a part of it. She was close in case Lara needed her.

Bianca settled into the chair. She wasn't used to having a third person in the room unless she was interviewing a couple, but if this was the only way Lara would agree to meet with her, then she would make it work. She studied Lara for a few minutes, trying to decide where to start.

"Lara, thank you for doing this."

"Sure, I'm happy to help. What would you like to know?"

"What are three words you would use to describe Ava?"

"Thoughtful, generous, and loving," Lara said very quickly.

"That was fast."

"It wasn't a hard question."

"Fair enough. Tell me why you picked those three words."

"Ava travels all over the world for her music, so I don't get to see her as often as I'd like, but every time she comes to London or we travel to one of her shows, every single time she has something for me. Usually something she saw that made her think of me, a particular book she thought I'd like or special picks for my guitar. So, even though we don't spend a lot of time together, I know that she loves me. If she didn't she wouldn't bother to show up for every birthday and special occasion. Her schedule is full, but she's always made time for me."

"I think those words fit her perfectly too. Okay, let's move on," Bianca said.

Ava couldn't quite believe her ears. She had no idea the little gifts and trinkets she'd brought Lara over the years had made such an impact. They were things she'd found and bought out of love for Lara. It was nice to hear they resonated for Lara as well.

She was also impressed with how Lara was handling the interview. She had grown up so much and Ava had been too busy to notice that she was virtually an adult fully capable of making her own decisions. She was glad she'd thought to give Lara a choice to do this interview or not.

Maybe she didn't have to worry so much about Bianca being around. Although she was still afraid her guilt would make her say something she would later regret. For now, she knew she had to continue to keep her distance. But damn if it wasn't eating her up. She wanted more than anything for things with Bianca to go back to the way they'd been at the beginning of the tour.

She knew that wasn't possible. At least not until she was able to tell her the truth. *Will Bianca ever understand why I gave up my daughter?* Not for the first time since she'd reconnected with Bianca, Ava wondered what her life would be like if she'd made different choices when she was younger. She had begun questioning everything.

The next morning a summer storm raged outside Bianca's bedroom window. The clash of thunder and flash of lightning woke her from a deep sleep. As soon as she realized what the sounds and lights were that disturbed her, she was able to calm her racing heart. She pulled the covers her head as she realized her sightseeing plans were a no-go for today. She'd have to think of something to do inside. Maybe she'd read for a bit. She had been looking forward to reading the latest Aurora Rey story.

She flung off the covers, climbed out of bed, and pulled on her robe. She found the book and curled up in the wingback chair. As she turned the page, she heard something that intrigued her. She would know Ava's music anywhere now. What was she doing playing so early in the morning?

She grabbed her key card. She was surprised to find the door of Ava's suite wide open. From the hallway she could see Ava facing the door, her eyes closed tightly. She was playing as though her life depended on it. Bianca knocked on the open door so she wouldn't startle Ava. There was no reaction as though Ava didn't hear the knock at all. Bianca stepped through the door and slowly approached Ava.

As she walked farther into the room, Bianca realized Lara was nowhere in sight, and the heavy curtains were pulled to cover the sliding glass doors like someone was trying to block out the thunderstorm. While Bianca could still hear the storm outside, she saw nothing except the occasional flash of light around the edges of the drapery. She stopped a few feet from Ava and tried to call her, but there was still no response.

She didn't want to startle Ava so she simply stood and listened to the music pouring out. Once the song ended, Ava opened her eyes and jumped at the sight of Bianca.

"I'm so sorry. I didn't mean to frighten you," Bianca said.

"What?" Ava asked.

"I said I'm sorry."

"Wait," Ava said. She put down her violin and bow and pulled earplugs from her ears. "What?"

"I'm sorry I frightened you."

"Oh. I'm fine."

"Why are you wearing earplugs to play the violin?"

"I'm not. I'm playing the violin because the earplugs didn't totally help."

"Help what?"

"Block out the storm. I'm not very fond of thunder."

A loud clap made Ava jump again and she looked longingly at her instrument as though seeking comfort.

"Hey, Ava, look at me," Bianca said. "Look into my eyes."

Ava did as instructed. "That helps some." Ava didn't jump as badly during the next clap of thunder. Bianca took her hand and led her to the couch.

"Talk to me. I didn't know you were scared of thunderstorms."

"I usually block out the fear. I don't even like to think about it or I pretend it's not true, which works as long as we're not in the middle of a thunderstorm."

"Sure. Keep looking at me. Nothing in this room is going to hurt you."

"Maybe we could talk about something else to get my mind off the weather?"

"Of course we can. Anything you want," Bianca said.

"How about paella?"

"I love paella."

"Me too."

"No, I don't think you understand how much I love paella. It may be my favorite food in the whole world aside from my mother's cooking," Bianca said.

"I can relate. I've been all over the world and I try to find the best paella restaurants I can."

"Really? How am I just hearing about this now? I've never found anyone who enjoyed paella as much as I do."

Ava reached for her tablet. "I can prove it. I take pictures of all the different paellas and the places I have them, so I can go there again if it's worth having."

They scrolled through the pictures for a few minutes as Ava described the places and flavors of some of her favorite paella experiences.

"Where is the best place for paella in London?"

"What's in it for me if I tell you?" Ava asked playfully.

"Anything you want." For the first time in weeks, Bianca felt like they were really clicking again. This is what the first few weeks of their trip had been like, playful and carefree. She missed the easy conversations and it was nice to be feeling this again.

"Really? What if I just take you there?"

"Come on, Ava, you have to tell me. You can't keep something like that all to yourself. Tell me the secret."

"All right, all right. But you must promise to keep it to under wraps. If too many people find out, it could make things difficult."

"I promise."

"Okay, the truth is—"

"I can't believe you're going to tell her when we just agreed yesterday that would take the story out of our hands," Lara shouted.

Ava whirled around and stood up. She tried to block Bianca from the anger she saw on Lara's face. She replayed the last couple sentences in her head and knew what Lara must be thinking. "Lara, this is not what you think it is. We were talking about—"

"It's obvious what you were talking about. How could you do this without checking with me?"

"No really, Lara, I promise we weren't." Ava looked at Bianca who wore a look of surprised confusion. "Bianca was just asking me—"

"I heard what she asked you. She wanted to know your secret and you were about to tell her I'm—"

"Lara, stop!"

"—your daughter."

An eerie silence descended on the room. Even the storm seemed to be holding its breath. Bianca got to her feet. She looked at Ava and then she turned to Lara. "Excuse me, you're her what?"

"Bianca, I can explain," Ava said.

Bianca didn't look at her; she continued looking at Lara.

Lara looked between the two of them, the fight seeming to have drained from her. Then she raised her head and looked directly at Bianca. "I'm her daughter. That's what she was about to tell you."

"Actually, she was about to tell me about the best place in London to find paella."

"Paella?"

"Yes, but I guess I'll have to find out about that another time as it seems the two of you may need to talk." Bianca headed for the still open door.

"Bianca, wait," Ava said, more panicked than she was during the thunderstorm.

Bianca turned to Ava again. "Clearly, you and Lara need to figure some things out. I don't want to get in the way."

"We should talk," Ava said. She looked at Lara, and her concern for her overrode everything else. "Soon, we should talk soon."

"I'm all talked out right now anyway," Bianca said. "I need some time." She walked across the hall and let herself into her room.

Ava wanted to go after Bianca but she couldn't. She had to take care of Lara who stood staring after Bianca. Lara looked shell-shocked. Ava closed the suite door and then she stepped to Lara. "You all right?"

"Were you…?" Lara began.

"What?"

"Were you two really just talking about paella?"

"I'm afraid so." Ava walked to the couch and collapsed into the cushions.

Lara sank down beside her. "Well, I've gone and made a bloody mess now haven't I?"

"You didn't do anything wrong."

"What do you think she's going to do with the information?"

Ava wished she knew the answer to that. She wanted to believe Bianca wouldn't hurt her or Lara. At the very least she wanted to believe that Bianca would talk to her before doing anything else. But Ava couldn't really understand the expression on Bianca's face when she left the room. She had an uneasy feeling, but she didn't want to scare Lara. "I don't know."

"I've ruined everything haven't I?"

"Yesterday you were considering telling people. Is this really so bad?"

Lara seemed to consider the question before answering. Then she shrugged. "I guess not. Because you're right, after we talked, I told my best mates and they're cool with it. I don't really care what anyone else thinks." Lara looked relieved at the realization.

"Then I guess you haven't ruined anything, have you?"

"What about Bianca? She didn't look happy when she left."

"You let me worry about that," Ava said. And worry she did. Lara had dropped a major bomb on Bianca, and Ava had no idea how she would react to the news. She had seemed a bit defeated and a lot disappointed when she left. The defeated part didn't make any sense to Ava. She looked over at Lara. "Maybe I'll go check on her."

"She said she was all talked out. Maybe you want to give her some time."

Damn, the kid is smart. "Perhaps that would be best." But Ava didn't have to like it. She wanted to go deal with it right now and figure out where things stood with them. Lara was right though. Bianca had asked for space and she had to give her that.

Bianca walked into her room and shut the door, then she just stood and stared into the dim room. While the thunderstorm outside seemed to have passed, a heavy gloom shrouded the room. It matched her mood perfectly. She had no idea what to do next. Lara was Ava's daughter. *Holy shit! How did I not see that?* As she thought about it now, all the pieces started to fall into place. She finally knew who Damon Blake was to Ava. The timing fit. He had to be Lara's father. She had so many questions. Not just for Ava. She had plenty for herself too.

How could she have been so blinded by her relationship with Ava that she hadn't figured out this whole scenario on her own? If she'd been clear-headed and not absorbed in her subject she would have figured out what Ava was keeping from her. She had wanted to give Ava the benefit of the doubt that she would have eventually told her the truth. On some level, she understood why Ava kept it from her. On the other hand, it hurt her deeply. Even when they'd talked about the child Bianca has lost, Ava never once mentioned she had a daughter.

Even now knowing the truth, she was certain she would never write a word about it if Ava asked her not to. It made her question her professional ethics. They had made an agreement that she would work on an article, but always in the back of her mind Bianca had been working with the goal of the biography. As a biographer, her job was to be an objective observer. She had built a reputation as someone who told the complete story, even revealing the hidden secrets.

She had failed on every front in this case. She was so disappointed in herself. Nobody would take her seriously as a biographer who told in-depth stories if the truth ever came out about Ava and Lara and she hadn't written about them. But she couldn't write the story and risk hurting Ava. No project had ever made her doubt her integrity before. She did not like the feeling.

She didn't know how she could have let it get this far. She knew why it happened; she was in love with Ava. What she should have done, when she realized that, was beg off the project and go home. Not try to continue to make it work. She had been unable to walk away then. Perhaps she could be stronger now. One thing was clear. She needed to actually talk to Ava.

CHAPTER NINETEEN

When Bianca's phone chimed to remind her of the lunch appointment she had set with Ava the day before, she considered not going. She needed more time to process what she had learned. In the end, she decided it was more important to talk with Ava. Once she had more answers, it might be easier to sort through her tangled thoughts.

As arranged, Bianca knocked on Ava's door promptly at noon. Ava opened the door. "Hi, I wasn't sure you'd come."

"I wasn't sure either, but here I am. We need to talk."

"I know we do. I asked Vicki to cancel our reservations. I thought it might be easier to talk here."

"Okay," Bianca said.

"Shall I order up some food?"

"I'm not hungry, but go ahead if you'd like."

"I don't think I could eat anyway. Would you like to sit?"

"Sure." Bianca chose the chair. She needed the space and distance from Ava right now.

Ava remained standing. "Can I least get you something to drink?"

"No, thank you. I just need to know—"

"What? I'll explain anything you want."

"Was any of this real?" Bianca gestured between the two of them.

"How can you ask me that?"

"Well, the way I figure it, you were lying or at the very least knowingly withholding information from me from the day we began this trip. So, what am I supposed to think? You played me like a fiddle and I just went right along with it."

Bianca's words stung, and Ava had to take a moment, lest she respond in anger. She took a deep breath. "What are you talking about?"

"Because of our relationship, I let your secret be just that. As a writer, it's my job to get the real story, to find the truth. I didn't even try to look for it because I didn't want to overstep, and you asked me, you played on my sympathies and you begged me not to dig too deep. I never should have been in that position."

"I'm sorry, Bianca. I wanted to tell you about Lara from the beginning. I had only ever told one person in my life besides my parents, and it was too hard to say the words out loud. If I'm being completely honest, there was a part of me that was scared you would hate me if you knew I'd given up my child when you'd never meet yours. Then, when I knew I had to tell you, when I felt it was important for you to know because keeping the secret was tearing me apart, it felt only fair that I tell Lara first."

"I get that on some level, I really do. What I don't understand is why go along with even pretending you were considering having your biography written when you were never going to let that happen? You couldn't. It would threaten your secret."

"It was the only way to convince you to stick around." Ava spoke without thinking and as soon as the words left her mouth she knew she'd made a fatal error.

Bianca stood. "So it was all a ploy from the very beginning."

"That's not what I meant." Ava tried to backpedal.

"Well, haven't I just been the fool? You got to have your fun and now you get your wish; your biography will not be written, at least not by me." Bianca started walking toward the door.

The sadness in Bianca's voice put Ava on high alert. This is not how this was supposed to go. She was losing ground and she had no idea how to stop the slide. "Bianca, please don't go. Let's talk about this."

Bianca whirled around, and Ava could feel the anger pulsing off of her. "Every time I talked about the daughter I would never know, you had an opportunity to tell me your story, and every time you made a choice not to."

"You have to know that I wanted to."

"How could I possibly know that? It seems there's a lot I don't know about you. This makes me question everything I thought I knew. What is left to talk about?"

"I care about you," Ava said.

Bianca laughed joylessly. "Is that what you call this? You can keep that kind of caring to yourself."

Ava was near panic as Bianca reached the door. "Wait!"

Bianca turned back.

"Please. Please give me another chance."

"What's the point?"

Ava didn't know what to say to that. There were many things she wanted to say, but she was scared. She was afraid that she would bare her soul and it wouldn't matter anyway. She said nothing. She was a coward.

"I'm going to go now." Bianca turned and walked out of the room.

Ava stared at the door that Bianca closed behind her. She hadn't missed the grief and hurt that crossed her face as they talked. That was her fault. She wanted to go after her and apologize again and beg for forgiveness, but it was hopeless. Maybe if she gave her a little time to cool off, they could talk again. Surely all they had shared was worth salvaging. She'd try again after the show tonight.

Hours later, Ava still couldn't get the sadness in Bianca's eyes out of her head. She had to go on stage in just a couple minutes. Talking to Bianca again would have to wait. She turned to the mirror to make sure everything was as it should be. She stretched her arms and fingers and picked up her violin. She was ready for her cue.

As she walked on stage she glanced at the seats where she expected Bianca, Lara, and Steven to be. She faltered for a fraction of a second when she saw Bianca's seat was empty. She made eye contact with Steven. He lifted his shoulders slightly and gently shook his head. She lifted the violin and began to play but her heart was in her throat throughout the entire performance. Where was Bianca?

Ava played flawlessly, but the music didn't infuse her soul with wonder as it usually did. Her concern rose by the minute. Bianca hadn't missed a single performance since Paris. Where was she? What was she doing? Ava played back their conversation from that afternoon. She had a bad feeling about this. She would find her as soon as she could and they would figure things out. She'd find a way to make this right.

Once Ava took her bows, she hurried to her dressing room. Moments later, Steven was there. "Where is she?"

"I thought you knew," Steven said.

Ava's stomach dropped. She hoped he wasn't saying what she thought he was. "Knew what?"

"She left."

"Well, I need to go see her. Can you cover for me with Hank so I can go to the hotel?"

"I would, hon, but she didn't just go back to the hotel. She said she was going home."

"What? Why?" Ava started to panic. She had to calm down and figure this out.

"She said you talked earlier today and you knew she was leaving," Steven said.

Ava thought about Bianca's last words. "Bullocks. Do you think I can still catch her?"

"No idea, but I don't know why you're still here if you're going to try."

"Will you…"

"I'll make sure Lara gets back to the hotel, ask Vicki to take care of your violin, and make up an excuse for Hank. Just go," Steven said.

"Thanks." Ava didn't even bother changing out of her gown. She grabbed her wallet and phone and then headed to the nearest exit so she could catch a cab.

She flagged down a taxi and gave the driver the address, imploring him to hurry. She tried to call Bianca. It went directly to voice mail. She hung up. She knew she should leave a message, but she wasn't sure what she wanted to say. She felt sick.

She tried calling her again. This time when it went to voice mail she was ready. "Bianca, please don't run away. Don't throw this away. I think we could have something really good here. Please at least stay and hear me out."

Ava raced to Bianca's hotel room. She took a deep breath before she knocked. She needed to calm down. It didn't matter. There was no answer. She knocked again. Harder. "Bianca! If you're in there please open up, I need to talk to you."

Nothing.

Ava leaned her head against the door. She couldn't think. Bianca was gone and it was her own damn fault. She didn't know what to do next. She went to her room. She left the lights off and used the faint light filtering through the curtain to walk to the chair without hitting her shins. Not that it mattered. She was numb. She collapsed onto the chair and stared straight ahead. What was she going to do now?

Ava had no idea how long she sat there. Her mind consumed with thoughts of Bianca. Finally, she heard knocking. She jumped up hoping Bianca had come back. She rushed to the door and pulled it open. Steven and Vicki stood there. She didn't say anything. She left the door open and walked back to the chair where she crumpled into it once again.

"I'm guessing you didn't catch her," Steven said as he flipped on the lights.

Ava blinked in the sudden brightness. "You'd be correct. Is Lara okay?"

"She's fine. We told her the same story we told Hank. You're ill. She's happy to watch movies in Vicki's room for the night."

"Thanks."

"What's this?" Vicki asked, indicating the desk across the room.

"What's what?" Ava tried to see the desk without moving from her chair.

"There are three envelopes here and the phone I gave Bianca to use while we're in Europe. The envelopes are for you, me, and Hank."

"What's in yours, Vic?" Steven asked.

"It looks like her room card, the airport lounge card, and a note that says: 'You're very good at your job. Thank you for everything you did for me.'"

Steven picked up the envelope addressed to Hank. "This isn't sealed, should we take a peek?"

"Yes," Vicki said.

Steven looked over to Ava who observed silently. She nodded. "Go ahead."

"There's a note and a check." He read the note to himself. "Apparently, Bianca felt since she wouldn't be writing the book, she should return the entire advance."

"She would," Ava said flatly. She wondered briefly what Bianca would do about the article. They'd never signed any paperwork. At least not that she knew about. Maybe Bianca was free to sell as many articles as she wanted to whomever she wanted. It didn't really matter now.

Vicki handed Ava the envelope with her name on it. A part of her wanted to wait and look at whatever was inside when she was alone. But Steven and Vicki were her two closest friends and she'd eventually tell them what it said anyway. She braced herself and took out the single sheet of paper.

Ava,

I leave with a heavy heart. Please know that I enjoyed the time we spent together. I feel bad about leaving this letter rather than talking to you in person. Given our last conversation, I don't think there's much left to say. I'm sorry our time was cut short. I had hoped to spend many more weeks getting to know you and your story. It's a story that I cannot in good conscience write any more. I feel it's best for me to return home. I wish you and Lara the best of luck in truly getting to know each other with nothing standing between you. I sincerely hope you find peace in the future.

Bianca

Ava laid her head on the back of the chair and dropped her hand to her lap. "Well, I guess that's that."

"How can you say that?" Steven asked.

"What else would you like me to say? She's gone."

"So go and get her back. You care about her. Isn't she worth fighting for?"

"It wouldn't do any good. She thinks I'm a liar and a manipulator. Damn it. I couldn't have made a bigger mess if I'd tried." She took a deep breath. "I need time to think. Please, go."

Steven tried again. "Ava…"

She held up a hand. "Not now."

Once they left, Ava threw the door latch, turned off the lights, stripped out of the gown she still wore, and collapsed onto the bed. She had never hurt so much in her life.

CHAPTER TWENTY

Nothing was the same for Ava. When Bianca left, almost everything in Ava's life dimmed. Bianca had been gone for three weeks. Instead of the pain fading, it seemed to be getting worse. *I completely let her down. She believes I was just using her.* These thoughts played in an endless loop in Ava's head every time she thought about Bianca and why she'd left. Ava didn't know how to fix things or if she could. She had done nothing to inspire trust.

She hid a massive secret from the woman she loved. *Holy hell.* It was true though. Ava knew it without a doubt. She loved Bianca. Even if she hadn't been aware of it when she hadn't shared her secret, it was also true then. The fact that she was keeping a promise to Lara did not exonerate her from not being honest with Bianca. Besides, she had known Lara was becoming more comfortable and she probably could have convinced her to let her tell Bianca. It was her own fear that had stopped her.

Now she had to think of a way to get through to Bianca. She wasn't responding to emails or phone calls. She only hoped that she was reading the emails and listening to the voice mails, even if she wasn't answering them. She had to see Bianca in person. She needed to get Bianca to see her and hopefully listen. She knew a simple apology wouldn't be enough.

She considered leaving the tour early and flying to see Bianca. But she didn't want to make any rash decisions and let so many people down. She had to be responsible and take care of business first. She hoped when she finally got to see Bianca, she wouldn't be too late. Maybe they both needed some time.

She didn't get the same satisfaction from her music as she always had. Steven and Vicki were trying their hardest to pull her out of her funk, but she just wanted to be left alone. The only bright spot in her life was Lara. They were spending a lot of time together, and Ava was grateful Lara seemed to be as interested in having a real relationship with her as she did. Even now, as Lara sat on the other sofa with her ear buds in listening to something or other, Ava was glad to have her nearby. At that moment, Lara looked over.

"Can I ask you something?" Lara asked as she pulled her ear buds out.

"I think we've established you can ask me anything you want," Ava said.

"You seem really sad. Are you?"

"I am."

"Why?"

Ava thought for a moment. How much should she share? What she was feeling was a lot to drop on a teenager. Finally, she decided to keep it simple and let Lara direct the conversation. "I miss Bianca."

"But I thought you didn't want your biography written."

"The only real problem I had with it was I didn't want you to be hurt. But it's more complicated than that. Bianca wasn't just my biographer."

"What do mean? Oh, wait, like she was your girlfriend?"

"Yes. But it went deeper than that, at least for me. I really care about her."

"You love her."

"I do." It helped a little to admit it out loud.

"So what happened?"

"It's…"

"Complicated, I get it. So, break it down for me."

Ava studied Lara for several moments. "You're sure you want to hear all this?"

"I wouldn't have asked if I wasn't."

Taking Lara at her word, Ava began her story, from the first time she saw Bianca on the bench at Tanglewood. She told her about the two years where she thought about Bianca and wondered if she'd ever see her again. About her joy at seeing her from that same bench only a couple of months before. Then she shared with Lara what the past two months had meant to her. "I've never felt this way about another woman. I'm in love with her and I messed it all up."

"Because of me?"

"No, not exactly. You asked me not to say anything, and I wasn't willing to break my promise to you. I'm certain if that's all that was between us we could have made it work. Bianca also feels like she let her profession down by not digging in to uncover the real story of what I was hiding from her. She feels like she failed as a writer because she and I had a relationship."

"She shouldn't be so hard on herself. There's no way she could have figured out about us even if she'd done a ton of digging. Is there?"

"I don't know. She seems to think she could have found something. That she should have. That's a pretty high hurdle to overcome since nothing I can say will ever convince her otherwise. She did find out that I left school for a while, and I was the one that asked her not to look too hard into why."

"Is that what's standing between you?"

"It's part of it. The biggest problem, as I see it though, was I never told her how I felt about her. I was too scared. I have never said the words to anyone and I just couldn't convince myself that Bianca would want to hear them or could return the feelings. She said she wanted to keep things between us easy and light. They weren't light for me, even from the very beginning. I should have been honest with her from the start."

"So tell her now. Go fix it."

"It's not that easy."

"That's the same as saying it's complicated."

"Well, it is."

"What have you got to lose by telling her how you feel? You're pretty miserable right now. Even if she doesn't feel the same way, don't you want to know that? Don't you want to fight for what you want rather than wonder about what might have been your whole life…again?"

She did get it. "You make an excellent point."

"I know."

❖

Bianca briefly grieved the loss of her relationship with Ava. She wouldn't allow herself to wallow. She had only herself to blame. Nobody needed to know that she still thought of her often or that her heart ached when something sparked a memory of their time together.

Shortly after she left the tour, she wrote a series of profiles on Ava. While she would not be writing Ava's biography, she didn't want all she'd learned about the amazing woman and musician to go to waste. She steered quite clear of anything remotely close to Ava's family. The stories she wrote helped bring a bit of closure to her time with Ava.

A month after she returned home, Bianca decided she needed something new to focus on. She called Wren Stark.

"Hello?"

"Hi, Wren, it's Bianca Vega."

"Oh, Bianca, so nice to hear from you. Where are you these days?"

"I'm at home in Massachusetts."

"I'm surprised. I thought you would be touring for months yet."

"If I was still working on Ava's biography I probably would be. That project isn't going to pan out. It's a long story that I'd rather not get into right now."

"Okay, I understand. So, what can I do for you today?" Wren asked.

"Well, I have nothing on my schedule for the foreseeable future. I was wondering if you were still interested in having me ghostwrite your autobiography."

"Of course I am."

"Is now a good time to talk specifics or should we set up a meeting for that?"

"Now is as good a time as any. Let me just get a pad so I can take some notes."

Once they ironed out the details, Wren said, "I'll get this stuff over to my manager and have her send you the contract."

"Wonderful, thank you," Bianca said. "So, once that's all squared away, where do you want me to meet up with you?"

"Next Saturday there is a Women's Performers Gala in Atlanta. Why don't you fly in Friday afternoon and we'll have dinner? Then you can accompany me to the gala the next day. The real work can start the following Monday. How would that work for you?"

"One question, when you say 'accompany you to the gala' what do you mean?" Bianca didn't want there to be any misunderstandings, so it was best to ask for clarification rather than be stuck in the ambiguity.

"Oh, I meant strictly as a friend and as my ghostwriter. Having my story written is very important to me, and I wouldn't do anything to jeopardize that."

"I appreciate that. I'm sorry if that was rude, but after my last experience I just wanted clear expectations."

"Not rude at all. It's always good to know exactly where things stand. So, shall I have my assistant book your flight for Friday?"

"Yes, that sounds like a plan."

"I'll ask her to send you a copy of the rest of the itinerary so you know what to pack."

"Thank you. I'll see you Friday then."

"Wonderful. I'm looking forward to getting started."

CHAPTER TWENTY-ONE

The flight to Atlanta had been uneventful, and dinner with Wren the night before had been pleasant. Now, as Bianca dressed for the gala, she couldn't help but think of all the fancy events she'd attended with Ava. The gown she wore tonight was new, but she had worn many like it to accompany Ava to donor events and similar functions. She had to figure out a way to stop thinking about Ava and move on with her life.

There was a knock on the door and she opened it. "Good evening, Wren. Are you always so punctual?"

"Rarely, actually, but I'm excited about tonight and have been ready for a while. I'm totally going to fan girl all over Amy Ray and Emily Saliers."

"I see." Bianca grinned at Wren's excitement and grabbed her clutch. "Well, shall we go then?"

"Absolutely. You look beautiful, by the way."

"Thank you."

Since they were staying at the hotel across the street from the Fox Theater where the gala was being held, the trip was very short. Once they were inside, Wren turned to Bianca. "Would you like something to drink?"

"Sure. A white wine would be lovely. A Pinot Grigio or Sauvignon Blanc, preferably."

"On it."

While Wren was at the bar, Bianca took a few minutes to admire the decorating. The spaces she could see from this spot were glitzy and shiny, the perfect backdrop for a night celebrating women performers.

"Here you go."

Bianca turned to Wren and accepted the offered glass. "Thank you."

"You're welcome," Wren said absently as she looked at something over Bianca's shoulder. "Can I ask you a personal question?"

"I suppose."

"How did you leave things with Ava?"

"Do you want to get into that right now?"

"Well, not really, but since she just walked in, I hope you're at least on amicable terms. If not, I won't mind if you need to leave."

"I appreciate that. I might just need to. If I disappear, I'll catch up with you tomorrow."

"If you decide to stick around, save a dance for me, okay?"

"You got it."

Bianca finally turned around and saw Ava standing across the room. All the feelings she'd tried to bury came rushing back. Why hadn't she prepared herself better? How could she have? She didn't know Ava was going to be here. She should have at least known it was a possibility. She was a woman performer after all. Bianca had stopped following Ava's schedule after she left the tour. It was just too hard.

She was only kidding herself to think she was over Ava. She was still madly in love with her. There was too much between them though. It would never work. She offered a small smile in acknowledgement and then she turned away. Seeing Ava was too painful. She needed air. She quickly made her way to the open terrace doors.

As soon as Ava had walked through the doors, her gaze was drawn to Bianca. Before Bianca saw her though, she had turned around to accept a glass of wine from Wren Stark. Why were they here together? Had Bianca already moved on? Then Bianca turned around and met her gaze. She smiled briefly. Ava's heart lifted. Then Bianca turned and headed for the doors.

Watching her walk away again hurt Ava's heart. She wasn't going to let it happen this time without trying to change it. She followed Bianca outside. Once she realized Bianca had simply stepped out onto the terrace, Ava took a moment to catch her breath. Bianca was facing away from her. She walked over to Bianca and stood beside her. "Good evening, Bianca, what a pleasant surprise to see you here."

"Ava," Bianca said making only the barest hint of eye contact.

"Do you hate me so much you can't even look at me?"

Bianca did turn to her fully then. "I don't hate you."

Ava was relieved to hear that, but something was definitely going on. Bianca was different. "How are you? And the family?"

"I'm fine. My family is all well and yours?"

Ava hated the impersonal conversation, something she might share with a stranger. She had to get Bianca to talk to her like she used to. "Everyone is healthy. I saw you with Wren Stark earlier. Are you here together?" What she really wanted to ask is, "Are you together?"

"Yes, I'm here as Wren's guest."

"Oh." Ava wasn't sure what else to say. "Perhaps I should let you get back to her then." It was the last thing she wanted to do.

"It's not like that. I'm ghostwriting her autobiography. We are not *together*."

"Oh."

Bianca laughed. "I remember you having a much stronger vocabulary."

Ava's heart lifted hearing the humor in Bianca's voice. "I'm sure it's still here somewhere, I just…I'm not sure what to say to you."

"What do you want to say?"

"I want to say I'm sorry that things turned out the way they did. I miss you and I wish we could start over. Could we do that? Have a fresh start?"

"What do you mean?"

"Bianca, would you go on a date with me?"

"I'm sorry, Ava, I can't." She really did look sad about it.

"Okay, I guess I should leave you alone then." Ava had to get out of here before she turned to a pile of mush.

"Why? Surely after everything, we can still be friends, can't we?" Bianca asked.

"See, that's just it. I don't want to be friends with you or not just friends anyway. Bianca, I should have been honest with you before you started touring with us. When we agreed to keep our relationship easy and carefree, I should have told you then it never was for me."

"What do you mean?"

"From the day you came back into my life I began falling in love with you. Every day we spent together made that feeling grow. Every adventure we had it deepened. For the first time in my life I understood what all those happy love songs are about. Then, when you left, I realized why all the sad love songs have a place of their own. I was devastated.

"There is this hole in my heart and you are the only one that will fill it. I am in love with you, Bianca. I'm sorry you don't feel the same way, but I understand. Or at least I'll try to. Now maybe you can see why we can't be friends, at least not yet. I need some more time to get over you. I'm going to go." Ava turned away from Bianca.

Bianca laid a hand on her arm. "Wait."

"What?"

"Are you messing with me right now or did you really mean what you just said?"

"I meant every word."

Bianca stepped into Ava's space leaving only a hair's distance between them. "Then you should kiss me now."

"But..."

"Kiss. Me."

Ava lifted her hand and cupped Bianca's cheek. She caressed her lips with her thumb. Then she moved her hand to her neck and bent forward slightly. She gently traced Bianca's lips with her tongue and then she kissed her deeply and thoroughly.

When Ava lifted her head, her eyes were dark and full of questions. "I'm confused. Was that good-bye?"

"If you truly meant what you said, I'd say it's hello."

"I don't understand. You said you couldn't go on a date with me, so where does that leave us?"

"Ava, darling, that was before I knew how you felt. I'm so deeply in love with you that the idea of going back into something casual with you was simply too difficult to consider."

"Wait, what did you just say?"

"Ava, I'm in love with you."

"Oh, thank the goddess. I love you so much, Bianca."

"I'll never get tired of hearing that."

"I'll never tire of saying it."

They stood and looked at one another for several moments as the emotions washed over them. Ava finally broke the silence. "What do we do now?"

Bianca held out her hand. "Now we dance."

EPILOGUE

Two years later

"Ava, are you ready?" Bianca asked from the doorway of their bedroom.

Ava laid down her hairbrush, and then spun on her seat to face Bianca. "Come here, sweetheart."

Bianca walked to Ava and looked down at Ava in her fitted tuxedo jacket. "Hi, wife."

"You'd think after a year, I'd get tired of that, but I still love hearing it."

"Good, because I love saying it and I don't plan on stopping anytime soon."

"How are you feeling?" Ava asked.

"Really good, the morning sickness seems to be behind me," Bianca said.

"I'm so glad." Ava leaned forward and kissed Bianca's abdomen. "Thank you for taking it easy on your mama, little one. You grow strong and healthy in there." When Ava looked back up, Bianca's eyes shone. "You okay?"

"I'm so happy and so in love with you. You're going to make a wonderful mum."

"I sure hope so, but I'm glad we're in this together."

"Forever and always. Now, before you stall any longer, are you ready? Everyone will be waiting for the star of the show."

Ava stood but kept hold of Bianca's hips. "Ready as I'll ever be. But I wouldn't mind a kiss for luck."

"There's an endless supply of those."

"Thank goodness." Ava leaned into Bianca.

"How are you feeling?" Bianca asked once they were in the jeep and on their way.

"Excited but nervous."

"I would be surprised if you weren't."

"Yeah, I'm sure somebody's going to want me to give a speech and you know how much I dislike talking in front of large groups of people."

Bianca rubbed Ava's thigh. "Try to remember that everyone there is someone near and dear to both of us. They all love you and want to see you succeed. And if it helps, just make eye contact with a few select people while you're talking and imagine you're only talking to them in that moment."

"Brilliant. I'll do that."

Bianca pulled the jeep into the studio parking lot. "Okay, deep breath, you've got this."

"As long as you're next to me, I can handle anything."

Ava meant those words from the bottom of her heart, but when they stepped through the door, she wasn't totally sure they were accurate. She was overwhelmed by the number of people who had come to show their support. Family and friends had flown in from around the world to help her launch her new venture.

She needn't have worried. Mere moments after she and Bianca walked through the door, Vicki was in front of them. "Champagne for you." She handed a glass to Ava. "And sparkling cider for you." She handed a matching glass to Bianca.

Ava took a large sip of the gold courage. "Thank you, Vicki. You're a lifesaver, as usual."

"My pleasure."

"You know you're under no obligation to take care of my every need anymore."

"It's a hard habit to break, but I'll try to leave it to your new assistant from now on."

"Good, you'll be too busy in your new role anyway. Besides, I'm counting on you to take care of all the details, when Bianca and I have to travel. It may not be as often as before, but I'm still committed to a few trips a year. So, you'll have to take care of everything here."

"About that…"

"Hang on, partner, let's leave business talk until Monday unless it's urgent."

"It can wait. But I do love it when you call me partner. Now, I should let you mingle with the rest of our guests."

"I suppose." Ava glanced at Bianca who had watched the whole exchange. "You'll be close?"

Bianca leaned in and whispered, "Of course, darling. Right here if you need me." *But you won't. You've got this.* Ava had come a long way over the years. She was much more comfortable talking to people now than she realized. Given everyone in the room was already a friend, this would be a piece of cake for her. Bianca was so proud of her. She'd set out to make something and she'd worked hard to make her dream a reality.

"You still look at her like you did two years ago. You're absolutely glowing," Elena said.

Bianca turned toward Elena. "I'm even more in love with her than I was then."

"I know."

"I'm glad you could make it."

"How could I not? I did help make this happen you know."

"I know you did. Ava and I are both so grateful we had someone we could trust to help her set this up. It's nice to have a lawyer in the family."

"It looks like Ava's family all made it too."

Bianca glanced over to where Ava stood surrounded by her parents, Lara, and Damon. She waited a moment to see if Ava needed her. Ava met her gaze with a smile. She was fine. "Yes, she's really excited that Lara's decided to attend college here after her gap year. She'll only be an hour away. I suspect we'll see a lot more of her parents now, especially with the baby coming. Her mom has talked about coming over for months at a time and with her dad so close to retirement, I wouldn't be surprised if they relocated at least temporarily until Lara figures out what she wants to do after college."

"I bet you'll see a lot more of Mom and Dad for a while too, once the little one arrives."

"That will be fun. It's probably a good thing we bought the bigger house."

"Absolutely."

They both looked over when someone started tapping the microphone to make sure it was live. Vicki spoke into it. "Ava, it's time for you to give that speech you'd rather not give." A ripple of laughter moved throughout the room. Ava looked to Bianca who nodded and walked toward the front of the room to be near while Ava spoke. Ava took the microphone from Vicki.

"You're a partner in this. Why am I the one who has to give the speech?"

Vicki grinned. "Because the whole thing was your brilliant idea."

"Right, that." Ava turned to the crowd. "Welcome, everyone, thank you for joining us in celebrating the launch of our new recording studio and music school."

Light applause erupted around the room.

"As Vicki so gallantly pointed out, this idea started with me, but it never would have come to fruition without the tremendous effort of so many of you in this room. Thank each of you who had a hand in making this dream of mine into a reality. I can't possibly thank each of you as much as I'd like, but I do need to extend an extra special thanks to a couple of women here. If it hadn't been for my partner, Vicki, and our amazing lawyer, Elena, we wouldn't be where we are today. Their tireless determination turned the spark of an idea into the brilliant fully formed studio and classroom you see around you. Vicki and Elena, thank you from the bottom of my heart." They all exchanged hugs as the room filled with applause. "Now, Bianca, would you come up here, please?"

Bianca took the few steps necessary to be at Ava's side. "My amazing wife, Bianca, was the first one I shared this idea with. She never let me brush it aside or give up on it. Her encouragement and support is why I'm here today. Bianca, thank you for being the best part of my life and for loving me, forever and always. I love you."

Bianca leaned in and whispered, "You nailed that speech, babe. I will love you, always."

Ava's smile was brilliant. She cleared her throat. "Now that I've made it through the speech portion of the evening, what do you say we get this party started?"

The crowd cheered.

"If you'll indulge me, I'll like to play one song for you that I've written for Bianca. This is the first time she will hear it."

Bianca whispered, "What did you do?"

Ava kept addressing the crowd. "After that, the band will take over and we can dance the night away. Let's celebrate the reason we're all here, music. Thank you, all, again for coming and supporting us. Please enjoy yourselves tonight."

When Ava placed the microphone back in its stand, Vicki appeared at her side with her violin. "Thanks, Vic." She lifted the violin, looked directly at Bianca, and began to play.

Every time Ava played her violin, Bianca was in awe of her talent. Having her play a song she wrote for her, that was beyond overwhelming. As Bianca listened to the rise and fall of the notes, the waves and crests of the melodies, her heart expanded and her love for Ava grew bigger and deeper. She laid her hands on her abdomen, making a connection with their unborn child. She was overpowered by the emotion Ava conveyed with her instrument. As the last note faded, she closed the distance between them. She pulled Ava into a soft kiss. "Thank you, that was beautiful."

"You're crying."

Bianca felt her face and wiped away the moisture. "Happy tears, darling, such happy tears."

"Well, all right then."

"Would you dance with me?"

"I will indeed, but first I promised the band, I would play one song with them. Then I'm yours for the rest of the night."

"You're going to play drums right now?"

"I was planning to, if you don't mind."

"I don't mind, darling. You're mine for the rest of our lives."

"I will never forget that."

Bianca walked away to find another drink while Ava got settled behind the drums. Elena found her as the bartender was handing her a club soda. Together they walked to the side of the room.

Elena looked toward Ava and back to Bianca. "Do you still get hot when she plays?"

"Every single time and now she's going to play drums. I don't think you've seen this yet. Brace yourself. Just thinking about it turns me on. She's going to have to take me home soon."

Elena laughed. "Perhaps I should go find Vicki and ask her to dance."

"You're a very smart woman."

Bianca watched from the sidelines as couples started to gather on the dance floor. Ava had encouraged her to follow her own dreams. Her second romance novel was due out any day now. Ava was her biggest supporter. She was fortunate for so many reasons and she would never take that for granted.

She focused on Ava as she played the drums with her heart and soul. She was married to a woman whose talent could not be contained by a single instrument. Luckily, Ava had made peace a long time ago, with both parts of herself. She no longer denied the rocker part of her soul. She loved both the violin and the drums and now she was free to play them both anytime she wanted.

By the time Ava finished playing the one song on the drums Bianca was so hot she downed her club soda in one gulp, trying to get a handle on the flames. The embers threatened to become a raging inferno when Ava wrapped her arms around her from behind and gently kissed her neck. "Are you ready for that dance? I'm all yours."

Bianca pulled Ava's hands down to her abdomen, so they were both connected to their baby. "Yes, you are. But I need a moment before I can dance. You make me so hot when you play."

"Take all the time you want, as long as I don't have to go anywhere."

"Oh, I'm counting on you holding me up."

"You got it."

Bianca gasped. "Did you feel that?"

"Was that…?"

"The baby's first kick, you did feel it." Bianca turned to face Ava. The look of shocked wonder made Bianca's heart melt. She wound her arms around her neck and leaned in for a gentle kiss.

Once they came apart, Ava laid her hand gently back on Bianca's stomach. "Wow."

"You seem so surprised. Don't you remember what it was like to have Lara kick when she was inside you?"

Ava's lips turned down at the corners. "Sure, but I was afraid and sick with worry the entire pregnancy. I don't have very many, if any, happy memories of that time. So, this is all new to me. Being excited about this baby coming into our life, it's so good."

"It's all good. The baby, our life, our family, we have so many good memories to make."

"I like the sound of that."

"Me too. I'm ready for that dance now."

"Right this way, sweetheart. Your dance card is full."

"As long as it's with you, that's just the way I like it."

The End

About the Author

TJ Thomas lives in western Massachusetts where she enjoys a quiet life with her college professor wyf, Elle, and their animals. TJ works in IT by day, but her passion is writing, and she spends much of her free time in that pursuit.

TJ and Elle are equidistant from their two adult children who live in London and San Diego, and they enjoy traveling to all points in between and beyond.

Books Available from Bold Strokes Books

A Chapter on Love by Laney Webber. When Jannika and Lee reunite, their instant connection feels like a gift, but neither is ready for a second chance at love. Will they finally get on the same page when it comes to love? (978-1-63555-366-6)

Drawing Down the Mist by Sheri Lewis Wohl. Everyone thinks Grand Duchess Maria Romanova died in 1918. They were almost right. (978-1-63555-341-3)

Listen by Kris Bryant. Lily Croft is inexplicably drawn to Hope D'Marco but will she have the courage to confront the consequences of her past and present colliding? (978-1-63555-318-5)

Perfect Partners by Maggie Cummings. Elite police dog trainer Sara Wright has no intention of falling in love with a coworker, until Isabel Marquez arrives at Homeland Security's Northeast Regional Training facility and Sara's good intentions start to falter. (978-1-63555-363-5)

Shut Up and Kiss Me by Julie Cannon. What better way to spend two weeks of hell in paradise than in the company of a hot, sexy woman? (978-1-63555-343-7)

Spencer's Cove by Missouri Vaun. When Foster Owen and Abigail Spencer meet they uncover a story of lives adrift, loves lost, and true love found. (978-1-63555-171-6)

Without Pretense by TJ Thomas. After living for decades hiding from the truth, can Ava learn to trust Bianca with her secrets and her heart? (978-1-63555-173-0)

Unexpected Lightning by Cass Sellars. Lightning strikes once more when Sydney and Parker fight a dangerous stranger who threatens the peace they both desperately want. (978-1-163555-276-8)

Emily's Art and Soul by Joy Argento. When Emily meets Andi Marino she thinks she's found a new best friend but Emily doesn't know that Andi is fast falling in love with her. Caught up in exploring her sexuality, will Emily see the only woman she needs is right in front of her? (978-1-63555-355-0)

Escape to Pleasure: Lesbian Travel Erotica edited by Sandy Lowe and Victoria Villasenor. Join these award-winning authors as they explore the sensual side of erotic lesbian travel. (978-1-63555-339-0)

Music City Dreamers by Robyn Nyx. Music can bring lovers together. In Music City, it can tear them apart. (978-1-63555-207-2)

Ordinary is Perfect by D. Jackson Leigh. Atlanta marketing superstar Autumn Swan's life derails when she inherits a country home, a child, and a very interesting neighbor. (978-1-63555-280-5)

Royal Court by Jenny Frame. When royal dresser Holly Weaver's passionate personality begins to melt Royal Marine Captain Quincy's icy heart, will Holly be ready for what she exposes beneath? (978-1-63555-290-4)

Strings Attached by Holly Stratimore. Success. Riches. Music. Passion. It's a life most can only dream of, but stardom comes at a cost. (978-1-63555-347-5)

The Ashford Place by Jean Copeland. When Isabelle Ashford inherits an old house in small-town Connecticut, family secrets, a shocking discovery, and an unexpected romance complicate her plan for a fast profit and a temporary stay. (978-1-63555-316-1)

Treason by Gun Brooke. Zoem Malderyn's existence is a deadly threat to everyone on Gemocon and Commander Neenja KahSandra must find a way to save the woman she loves from having to commit the ultimate sacrifice. (978-1-63555-244-7)

A Wish Upon a Star by Jeannie Levig. Erica Cooper has learned to depend on only herself, but when her new neighbor, Leslie Raymond, befriends Erica's special needs daughter, the walls protecting her heart threaten to crumble. (978-1-63555-274-4)

Answering the Call by Ali Vali. Detective Sept Savoie returns to the streets of New Orleans, as do the dead bodies from ritualistic killings, and she does everything in her power to bring them to justice while trying to keep her partner, Keegan Blanchard, safe. (978-1-63555-050-4)

Breaking Down Her Walls by Erin Zak. Could a love worth staying for be the key to breaking down Julia Finch's walls? (978-1-63555-369-7)

Exit Plans for Teenage Freaks by 'Nathan Burgoine. Cole always has a plan—especially for escaping his small-town reputation as "that kid who was kidnapped when he was four"—but when he teleports to a museum, it's time to face facts: it's possible he's a total freak after all. (978-1-63555-098-6)

Friends Without Benefits by Dena Blake. When Dex Putman gets the woman she thought she always wanted, she soon wonders if it's really love after all. (978-1-63555-349-9)

Invalid Evidence by Stevie Mikayne. Private Investigator Jil Kidd is called away to investigate a possible killer whale, just when her partner Jess needs her most. (978-1-63555-307-9)

Pursuit of Happiness by Carsen Taite. When attorney Stevie Palmer's client reveals a scandal that could derail Senator Meredith Mitchell's presidential bid, their chance at love may be collateral damage. (978-1-63555-044-3)

Seascape by Karis Walsh. Marine biologist Tess Hansen returns to Washington's isolated northern coast where she struggles to adjust to small-town living while courting an endowment for her orca research center from Brittany James. (978-1-63555-079-5)

Second in Command by VK Powell. Jazz Perry's life is disrupted and her career jeopardized when she becomes personally involved with the case of an abandoned child and the child's competent but strict social worker, Emory Blake. (978-1-63555-185-3)

Taking Chances by Erin McKenzie. When Valerie Cruz and Paige Wellington clash over what's in the best interest of the children in Valerie's care, the children may be the ones who teach them it's worth taking chances for love. (978-1-63555-209-6)

All of Me by Emily Smith. When chief surgical resident Galen Burgess meets her new intern, Rowan Duncan, she may finally discover that doing what you've always done will only give you what you've always had. (978-1-63555-321-5)

As the Crow Flies by Karen F. Williams. Romance seems to be blooming all around, but problems arise when a restless ghost emerges from the ether to roam the dark corners of this haunting tale. (978-1-63555-285-0)

Both Ways by Ileandra Young. SPEAR agent Danika Karson races to protect the city from a supernatural threat and must rely on the woman she's trained to despise: Rayne, an achingly beautiful vampire. (978-1-63555-298-0)

Calendar Girl by Georgia Beers. Forced to work together, Addison Fairchild and Kate Cooper discover that opposites really do attract. (978-1-63555-333-8)

Lovebirds by Lisa Moreau. Two women from different worlds collide in a small California mountain town, each with a mission that doesn't include falling in love. (978-1-63555-213-3)

Media Darling by Fiona Riley. Can Hollywood bad girl Emerson and reluctant celebrity gossip reporter Hayley work together to make each other's dreams come true? Or will Emerson's secrets ruin not one career, but two? (978-1-63555-278-2)

Stroke of Fate by Renee Roman. Can Sean Moore live up to her reputation and save Jade Rivers from the stalker determined to end Jade's career and, ultimately, her life? (978-1-63555-62-4)

The Rise of the Resistance by Jackie D. The soul of America has been lost for almost a century. A few people may be the difference between a phoenix rising to save the masses or permanent destruction. (978-1-63555-259-1)

The Sex Therapist Next Door by Meghan O'Brien. At the intersection of sex and intimacy, anything is possible. Even love. (978-1-63555-296-6)

Unforgettable by Elle Spencer. When one night changes a lifetime… Two romance novellas from best-selling author Elle Spencer. (978-1-63555-429-8)

Against All Odds by Kris Bryant, Maggie Cummings, M. Ullrich. Peyton and Tory escaped death once, but will they survive when Bradley's determined to make his kill rate one hundred percent? (978-1-63555-193-8)

Autumn's Light by Aurora Rey. Casual hookups aren't supposed to include romantic dinners and meeting the family. Can Mat Pero see beyond the heartbreak that led her to keep her worlds so separate, and will Graham Connor be waiting if she does? (978-1-63555-272-0)

Breaking the Rules by Larkin Rose. When Virginia and Carmen are thrown together by an embarrassing mistake they find out their stubborn determination isn't so heroic after all. (978-1-63555-261-4)

Broad Awakening by Mickey Brent. In the sequel to *Underwater Vibes*, Hélène and Sylvie find ruts in their road to eternal bliss. (978-1-63555-270-6)

Broken Vows by MJ Williamz. Sister Mary Margaret must reconcile her divided heart or risk losing a love that just might be heaven sent. (978-1-63555-022-1)

Flesh and Gold by Ann Aptaker. Havana, 1952, where art thief and smuggler Cantor Gold dodges gangland bullets and mobsters' schemes while she searches Havana' s steamy Red Light district for her kidnapped love. (978-1-63555-153-2)

Isle of Broken Years by Jane Fletcher. Spanish noblewoman Catalina de Valasco is in peril, even before the pirates holding her for ransom sail into seas destined to become known as the Bermuda Triangle. (978-1-63555-175-4)

Love Like This by Melissa Brayden. Hadley Cooper and Spencer Adair set out to take the fashion world by storm. If only they knew their hearts were about to be taken. (978-1-63555-018-4)

Secrets On the Clock by Nicole Disney. Jenna and Danielle love their jobs helping endangered children, but that might not be enough to stop them from breaking the rules by falling in love. (978-1-63555-292-8)

Unexpected Partners by Michelle Larkin. Dr. Chloe Maddox tries desperately to deny her attraction for Detective Dana Blake as they flee from a serial killer who's hunting them both. (978-1-63555-203-4)